MY FATHER'S JOY

A Story More Twisted than a Little Girl's Braids

Adapted from the Award-Winning Screenplay
GUNNAR E GARRETT JR.

ISBN-13: 9780692963944

ISBN: 0692963944

Library of Congress Control Number: 2017915806

BUGA Films, Oakdale, CA

For my daughters,

I want to thank you for always being supportive and proud of your father, even through my struggles in writing and life in general. I'll always be there for you as you have for me. And this book, though it's a twisted one, shows that there's nothing closer than family, regardless of the path you take or what the universe throws at you. Your daddy loves you!

Your father,
Gunnar E. Garrett Jr.

CHAPTER 1

THE HIPPIE COUPLE

On a quiet backcountry road deep in the hills of rural Alabama in 1976, crickets and bullfrogs echo throughout the night, not to be outdone by the fireflies flickering in the overgrown grasses beside the road.

A distant engine roar slowly begins to drown out the creatures of the night as headlights grow closer. The intensity of the headlights increases, but in a flash, they're gone as quickly as they appeared. The whining engine and taillights dissipate into the night as a Volkswagen van speeds past, leaving nothing but a cloud of dust that gradually settles.

Micah, who is behind the wheel of the van, is a fairly attractive young beatnik in his early twenties, with hair down to his shoulders and a week-old beard that should have been shaved before it got a chance to grow in splotches. With one hand on the wheel, he uses the other to brush his hair over his ear.

The driver's-side window is rolled down a smidgen, allowing Micah's half-buttoned, large-collared shirt to blow in the breeze as he methodically bobs his head to the distorted sound of Creedence Clearwater Revival flowing from the blown speakers of his van.

In the passenger seat, Victoria, a blond bombshell in her early twenties with a thin physique, minus her top-heavy bust, sways to the music as she rolls a joint in the top of a cookie tin.

The Volkswagen van drifts over the center line as Micah takes his eyes off the road to get a good look at Victoria and her progress.

"Would you just finish that fucking thing so I can smoke it already?" Micah says over the volume of the radio.

Victoria stops and lets her eyes roll in Micah's direction.

"Why don't you chill the fuck out? I'm almost done anyway," Victoria says, irritated with Micah's impatience.

"Bitchin'." Micah turns his attention back to the road, correcting the van's drift across the center line.

He lifts his foot from the gas pedal, and the needle on the speedometer slowly rotates counterclockwise as the van idles down.

"I'm gonna take a piss while you're finishing that thing." He leans forward, having held his bladder for quite a while.

"Right here?" Victoria's nervous about the lack of civilization.

"Yeah, right here," says Micah matter of factly. "Or you can hand me that bottle." He grins.

"You're such a fucking chump. Just pull over."

The whine of the tires on the blacktop is traded for the crunch of gravel on the shoulder as Micah guides the van to the side of the road. The front passenger tire slides to an abrupt stop, kicking up dust that floats out around the van and then slowly settles, revealing the Alabama license plate on the rear bumper.

Micah flings the driver's-side door open and hops out. He hurries around the front of the van, blocking the light from the headlights as he passes them on his way to the passenger's-side door.

Victoria rolls down her window as Micah approaches. He rests his forearms on the door and leans into the van.

"Why don't you do me a solid and be done with that by the time I get back?" he says with a smirk. "And, uh, maybe when I get back, I'll give you my solid."

Victoria quickly smacks his arm in a playful manner, only half-shocked by his comment.

"Fucking perv," she says, pretending to be offended but not fooling him. "Don't make me wait then." Her face lights up with a provocative smirk.

Micah stretches in to kiss Victoria. The kiss turns passionate as she grabs his face and kisses him with intent, making him yearning for more, and then pushes him away. She runs her tongue across her upper lip, leaving Micah breathless.

He reluctantly leans back from the window, gives the door a slap, and backpedals a few steps, pointing at Victoria and letting her know he's coming back to finish what they've started. He finally turns away and jogs into the woods.

"Don't fucking leave me here forever," Victoria yells as Micah disappears into the darkness.

Victoria slumps back into her seat, lets her head fall against the headrest, and gives an unsatisfied exhale, disappointed by the tease. Her eyes lock back on the cookie tin, and she sits back up, scooting into a better position to work with her joint.

She reaches for the radio, turning it up loud enough to drown out the sound of the night, and continues where she left off. Her head methodically sways forward and backward, keeping rhythm with the music as her fingers slide the rolling paper over the weed, packing it tight. Satisfied, she lifts the marijuana cigarette to her lips, runs her tongue along it lengthwise to wet the paper, folds it over, and presses it tight before spinning it between her fingertips and twisting the ends closed like a piece of dime-store candy.

Pleased with her work, Victoria places the joint between her lips, letting it dangle as she searches the glove box for a lighter. She finds one and strikes it. The flame radiates and reflects off her fair-colored skin, accentuating her high cheekbones and undeniable beauty. She lifts the flame to the joint and watches it bend, sucked to the tip of the joint by her deep inhale. The tip glows as the flame comes into contact with the joint, and the smoke recedes into Victoria's lungs. With a leisurely exhale, she lets a white cloud envelop the cabin of the van like fog settling in the San Francisco Bay on a winter's evening.

Head titled against the headrest and eyes closed, Victoria feels the music pulsing against her eardrums and the THC flowing through her body, allowing her to fade; her body relaxes, and her senses takes over, feeling the music from within. Taking another drag, she holds it in, exhaling only enough to let the smoke billow from her mouth while she presses the tip of her tongue to her upper teeth. When her body is starving for oxygen, she finally releases the remaining foggy haze that's thick enough to hide her face.

As the smoke slowly and steadily dissipates, the outline of a masked man begins to form over Victoria's shoulder in the far back seat of the van. She's oblivious. The man's eyes penetrate through eyeholes cut into the black burlap sack over his head. A red-painted frown below the eyeholes is sloppy, as if the artist couldn't wait to don the mask.

Far enough into the forest to not be seen yet close enough to keep the headlights of the van in view, Micah hides behind a thick bush and relieves himself. Finished, he shakes himself off and tucks everything back where it belongs. He zips his pants, buckles his belt, and gives his manhood an adjustment before he begins his trek back to the van. The interior light of the van shines like a beacon, guiding him back.

He spots Victoria resting her head against the passenger window as he approaches. An idea sparks, and he stops in his tracks. An obnoxious smile covers his face as he holds his laughter in and tiptoes near the rear of the van. He stoops low, keeping as quiet as he can as he closes in on the van, ducking behind it and slowly creeping his way up the side. He keeps his eyes focused intently on Victoria, hoping to maneuver his way to her without being seen.

Micah grins; he's managed to come within a foot of the window. With his back against the van, he spins, slapping both hands against the glass and screaming in hopes of scaring Victoria.

Puzzled by her nonresponse, he leans closer to take a good look. He reaches for the door handle, grips it tightly, and firmly presses his thumb against the release button.

Click.

The latch releases, and Victoria's limp body pushes the door open and slides from the seat. In a moment of natural reaction, Micah reaches to catch her before she falls, but the weight and awkward position are too much. Her body flops to the ground, with one leg still propped in the doorway.

"What the fuck?" Panicked, Micah takes a few steps back.

He's momentarily frozen. All he can do is stare at Victoria's awkwardly contorted body as it hangs halfway out of the van. Her head is twisted to the side and rests on the dirt shoulder of the road.

Blood spills from Victoria's neck, where a large slit stretches from her collarbone to her ear and down the left side of her body. Blood pools on the ground around her head. Micah can't help but think of a butchered hog.

Terrified and trembling, he steps back, trips over his own feet, falls, and rises just as quickly as he's fallen. Too preoccupied and scared to knock the dirt from his clothes, he spins back, ready to make a break for it, only to find himself face to face with the business end of a wooden Louisville Slugger en route to his jaw.

Crack!

The headlights of the Volkswagen van shine brightly into the distance of the backcountry road, while fireflies dance to the chirps of crickets that sing alongside croaking bullfrogs.

CHAPTER 2

A New Beginning

Two Weeks Earlier

A 1975 Ford Granada pulling a moving trailer packed full of boxes floats down a two-lane highway, passing a Welcome to Alabama sign.

Karen Cole, a thirty-seven-year-old soft-spoken woman of natural beauty—the kind whose makeup, if she wore any, would take from her aura—steers the land yacht of a car. Abby, her twelve-year-old daughter, rides shotgun, gazing out the window at the passing serenity of rural Alabama.

While she's in a daze, Abby's thoughts migrate far from where she's heading and back to where her story began. She mindlessly plucks at the ponytail holders around her wrist and then stops, only to begin fidgeting with the small silver trinity-shaped pendant that dangles from her neck, lightly stroking it between her index finger and thumb.

Karen shifts her eyes from the road to Abby, wondering where her daughter's mind has wandered.

"I see you're still wearing your father's charm," Karen says, momentarily pulling Abby from her thoughts.

"Yeah," Abby softly says. She lifts the pendant and twists it between her fingers as memories of her father return.

A warm smile remains on Abby's face as she turns her attention back out the window and watches the passing scenery. Her thoughts race back to what she remembers of times she shared with her father.

⁂

The familiar sounds of an unoiled, rusty chain on an old steel swing set reverberate through the local park, screeching with every back-and-forth motion of the swing.

Seven-year-old Abby's father, Eddie, a fairly attractive man in his early thirties, pushes her on the swing, barely able to concentrate on her as he looks into the distance.

Eddie's attention is focused on a young mother struggling to strap her toddler son into his stroller. Her frustrations mount as the toddler fights her tooth and nail, refusing to return to his seat.

"Dad," says Abby, trying once again to be the center of her father's attention.

Eddie snaps back from his daze, not realizing he had lost touch with reality and stopped pushing Abby long enough for her swing to have come to a complete stop.

"Oh, sorry. Let Daddy give you another push." Eddie grips the old rusted chains and pulls her back for another push.

"No, that's OK. I think I might go down the slide instead," says Abby with a subtle smile, her little mind wondering where her father's thoughts are.

"All right," Eddie says. He lowers the swing, allowing her to hop off.

As Abby skips off toward the slide, Eddie follows, though his attention is once again diverted by the uncontrolled outbursts of the toddler trying to claw his way from the stroller. Eddie stops in his tracks.

The young mother, irritated by not only the toddler and his behavior but also her own lack of control over her son, begins raising her voice loud enough for most of the park's patrons to hear.

"I swear to God. I am about to lose my shit!" She grasps the boy's arm and yanks him from the stroller. "This what you want? Fine."

Toddler in one hand and stroller in the other, the young mother drags both. The stroller skips and bounces until its wheels come off the ground, and the boy occasionally misses a step. The mother gives just enough of a tug to lift him from the ground and pull him back to her as she mumbles her way to a nearby brick outbuilding that houses the restrooms.

A solid, loud thump, followed by hysterical cries, reels Eddie back in from his daze. He spins back around to find a young boy lying in the fetal position at the base of the ladder leading up to the top of the slide.

As Eddie makes his way to the boy, who slowly lifts himself from the dirt and clutches his stomach in pain, he spots Abby standing tall atop the slide. Her arms are crossed, and a scowl covers her face as she looks down at what is clearly her victim.

Eddie reaches his hand out to the boy to help lift him. But once back on his feet, the sniveling boy pulls away. Fearfully he hobbles off, holding his arms against his stomach, crumpled over in pain.

"Abby, get down; we need to go," says Eddie. He fails to get a response from her, and she appears to be in a trance. Her scowl holds strong, and her eyes are locked on the boy fleeing into the distance.

"Abby!" Eddie finally gets her attention. She spins her head back toward her father.

Happy as a clam, bubbly Abby plops her rear end on the slide and coasts to the bottom, without a care in the world. Feet back on the ground, she meets her father at the base of the slide, and she grips his hand tight. Eddie escorts her from the playground as she skips at his side.

As Eddie and Abby head back onto the pavement and away from the playground, the vocal echoes of the young mother pour from the outbuilding.

Unable to ignore the cries of the child and ranting of the young mother, Eddie slows to a stop and looks down at Abby, who still has her hand in his. She gives a flicker of a smile up at him. Another outburst from the young mother draws their attention as they simultaneously turn back to the door of the outbuilding.

Eddie takes a knee, bringing himself down to Abby's level.

"Pumpkin, why don't you go wait on one of those benches over there, and I'll be back in just a minute."

With a nod and a radiant smile, Abby skips to a park bench. Eddie, a man who couldn't be happier to be a father, watches his cheerful little girl skip off in what feels like a slow-motion scene from a movie, and the world around him is silent, if only for the moment.

That moment is short lived.

The sights and sounds of the world around Eddie come back to him, almost closing in on him, as the cries from the brick outbuilding continue. The smile fades from his face, and a look of determination and hints of disgust begin to form.

As if there's work to be done, Eddie storms toward the outbuilding, with a steadfast stride of unwavering resolve. Without hesitation, he charges into the women's restroom and out of sight.

Patiently waiting on the nearby park bench for her father, her legs swinging back and forth inches from the ground, Abby stares up at a pair of blue jays nestled on a branch next to each other that are occasionally rubbing heads.

A scream rings out.

The birds spook.

Abby, semidisappointed, watches the birds spring from the branch and fly out of sight. Eyes still on the sky and hoping to spot the birds once more, she fails to see her father approach from behind and is startled when he places his hand on her shoulder.

Eddie takes his daughter's hand, and the father-daughter duo stroll down the paved path away from the playground, enjoying the warmth of the sun on their backs as they distance themselves from what Eddie felt had to be taken care of.

Behind them, back at the brick outbuilding, an unintelligible mumble and a cry leak from the ladies' room. From the doorway, the toddler staggers his way out, lost and alone.

᛭

Packed to the brim with cardboard boxes and other household goods, Karen's car slows and pulls to the side of the road, scraping the curb in front of a row of homes that are backed against a densely wooded area.

Abby, still lost in thought, blankly stares out the window at the row of houses, not realizing she's arrived at her new home.

"Abby," says Karen, trying to capture her attention.

"Huh?" Abby snaps out of the spell that most people fall under when forced to sit in a car on a cross-country drive.

"I said, 'We're here.'" Karen is surprised Abby didn't hear her the first time.

Abby smiles and turns back to look out her window, now actually acknowledging the home her mother's car is parked in front of. With a glance back at Karen, Abby climbs out of the car, excited for a new beginning.

Karen hops out of the driver's side and gazes over the roof of her car at their new home. She's excited and anxious to move on with her life, putting the past behind her and letting the future be unwritten.

"This it?" Abby asks, already knowing the answer.

Karen smiles and nods. "I think this will be nice, a fresh start, a new home."

"Looks good to me."

"Shall we?"

Karen motions toward the house, and Abby replies with a nod and a smile of her own. Karen walks around the car and holds Abby's hand tightly as the two prepare to take their first steps in the right direction. Hands clasped, Karen leads, with Abby skipping at her side.

As they approach the front door, Abby pulls the screen back and holds it as Karen slides the key into the lock and unlocks the door. As the keys dangle from the lock, Karen gives Abby one more excited glance, turns the knob, and lets the front door swing open.

With a sigh of relief, Karen steps through the threshold and into their new home.

CHAPTER 3

THE BOY NEXT DOOR

Inside Abby and Karen's new home, Abby wanders from room to room, curiously inspecting each one, until she comes to a long hallway. She pauses, though only momentarily, before continuing forward, letting her fingertips drag along the peeling wallpaper.

Abby slowly presses the doors of each room open, never entering, until she reaches the far room at the end of the hall. With her hand on the door, she gradually guides the door open, stands in the doorway, and investigates as much as she can without entering.

Satisfied she's seen as much as she can without stepping into the room, Abby lowers her head and stares at the floor, where the two different carpets have been joined together at the doorframe. Abby lifts her head and places her right foot forward, letting it land on the plush carpet inside the room.

With her feet fully planted on the floor of the bedroom, she rotates her head, scrutinizing every inch of the room and considering her possibilities.

Abby's eyes stop, drawn to a curtain-covered window. She steps forward, raises her hand to the fabric, and lets it slide back down gradually, like molasses.

"Abby, I'm gonna start grabbing boxes," says Karen, her voice echoing from another room.

Spooked, Abby yanks her hand back from the curtain.

"OK," she says, her eyes still admiring the extraordinary brown-and-orange paisley curtains.

Lifting her hands once again, Abby pulls back the curtains. Light pours into the room, brightening the already overpowering orange tones in the bedroom's carpet.

Abby stares out the bedroom window and across the way at the neighboring home's window. Astonished, she sees a young boy near her age staring back at her from his window.

Motionless, both children stare at each other, neither willing to break eye contact.

"Mom, I found my room," Abby yells, never letting her eyes stray from her target.

The boy, his eyes still locked on Abby's, raises one hand as if to wave but grabs the cord of his blinds. He pulls the cord, and the blinds drop, shielding him from view.

"What's that, Abby?" asks Karen.

Startled, Abby spins back to find her mother in the doorway of the bedroom.

"What are you looking at?" Karen enters the room and walks over to the window. She peeks out and sees nothing but the neighboring home.

"Nothing. I was just saying I found my room," Abby says.

"That was fast." Karen leaves the window. "Why don't you come help me grab some boxes?"

"Sure."

Karen exits the room to begin the tedious job of moving boxes in from her car. Abby begins to follow but then pauses for a moment before turning back to the window to take one last peek. Though the boy's blinds are still closed, Abby spots two fingers holding open a small section. Abby leans to catch a better glimpse, but the blinds snap shut.

"I need your help, Abby," Karen says from the other room.

"Sorry; I'm coming." Abby backs away from the window and hurries out of her bedroom.

Abby springs through the front screen door and lets it slam shut behind her. She sprints to her mother, who's standing on the walkway leading to the street and talking with a woman.

"There she is," Karen says as Abby approaches. "Abby, this is our new neighbor, Donna."

Donna appears to be about Karen's age. She flicks her cigarette, allowing the ashes to land by her feet. Her large sunglasses cover most of her face. Noticing Abby, she lowers her head and slides her shades down her nose, peering over the top of them to get good look at her.

"Hi. My name's Abigail. It means 'father's joy,' but everyone calls me Abby." Abby extends her hand to shake Donna's.

Donna and Abby shake hands. Abby takes a step back to her mother's side and reaches for the comforting feel of the pendant around her own neck, once again caressing it between her finger and thumb.

"Well, it's nice to meet you, Abby," Donna says in a deep Southern drawl, receiving a smile in return from Abby. "Just the two of you then? Or is there a mister?"

Karen, unsure of how to answer, glances down at Abby, who peeks back up at her before lowering her head and gripping her pendant tightly.

"He…uh…well, he's no longer with us," Karen says.

"Oh, Lord, I'm so sorry, sweetheart." Donna reaches out, rests her hand on Abby's shoulder, and rubs it gently. "If I had known, I wouldn't a said nothing."

"It's OK." Abby takes a deep breath and exhales with a sigh.

"My good-for-nothing husband left me and my son about two years ago. Said he was gonna head over to a friend's house—" says Donna, breaking off her sentence to take a deep drag from her cigarette. "I guess he forgot to mention his friend lives in Kentucky." She blows the smoke out of the side of her mouth, away from Abby. "And that she was a nineteen-year-old girl who was seven months pregnant with his child."

"How awful," says Karen, unsure how to take the mass of information that may have been a little much for a first meeting.

The trio wait in a short-lived, awkward silence while Donna takes another drag. Karen is able find a less personal topic of conversation.

"You said you have a son," she says, trying to pull from their earlier conversation. "How old is he?"

"Twelve." Donna looks at Abby and blows smoke from the side of her mouth. "Gotta be right about your age."

"Abby too," Karen says, excited about the possibility of her daughter finding a new friend.

"You wanna meet him?" Donna asks.

"Sure," Abby says happily.

Donna yells over her shoulder at the house. "Lucas! Go on and get your little ass out here!"

Abby lets a giggle slip at Donna's choice of words.

"So, what brings y'all out to Alabama?" Donna brings herself right back into the conversation as if she'd never stopped.

Karen shrugs. "I guess it was just time for a change. Right, Abby?" She figures she's found the most appropriate way to explain why she's moved her daughter across the country without divulging too much of her private life, unlike Donna.

Abby nods in agreement, knowing there's much more to their story than can ever be told or that she would even want to tell in one conversation, and especially not to someone whom she and her mother have met for the first time.

"There ain't no harm in that. A little change ain't never hurt nobody." Donna leaves the conversation where it lies.

Lucas comes outside and trudges toward his mother. His jeans are too short, and his shirt is bound to be a hand-me-down. Its loose fit and faded design could instantly advertise he's from the wrong side of the tracks, though his nearly new black high-top Converse shoes might say otherwise. But he could have picked them up at a yard sale. The heels scrape across the ground as he approaches.

"What?" he asks, irritated he's had to leave the comfort of his home, though he would most likely be irritated by anything his mother would ask of him.

"You better lose your attitude, boy. Now come on out here and meet our new neighbors. They came all the way out from California." Donna casually turns back. "Y'all ain't celebrities, are ya?" Her whisper hints she's excited to meet someone with any amount of fame.

Karen gives a halfhearted smile and shakes her head.

Lucas lifts his hand, gives a slight wave, and then spins back toward his house. He hopes he's not going to have to actually make conversation with anyone, particularly a new neighbor, and a girl at that.

"Boy, you better get your little ass back over here!" Donna's bark causes him to spin back around and head to her side. "He's got a bit of his father in him."

"I'm Abby," says Abby to Lucas as she extends her hand to shake his.

Rather than reciprocating, Lucas stands idle, doubtful she's worthy of returning the gesture. He blankly stares at Abby's outstretched hand, with no intention of shaking it.

Smack!

Donna strikes Lucas in the back of the head with the open palm of her hand. Lucas reaches for Abby's hand.

"Lucas," he mumbles, saying only the minimum needed to keep his mother from having another reason to lay one on him.

Abby and Lucas shake hands. Lucas then steps back to his mother's side and places his hands in his pockets, hiding them from the dangers of being shaken again by a stranger. He rolls his eyes to the top of his head, looking anywhere but at Abby and Karen to avoid any further conversation.

"I like your shoes," says Abby excitedly to spark some sort of real conversation.

Lucas glances down at his black high-tops and spots that Abby is wearing an identical pair, except that hers actually fit properly.

"It was nice meeting the both of you," Karen says. She places her hand on Abby's shoulder, breaking the ugly awkwardness typical of most children's first encounter with a new face. "Abby and I really should start bringing in boxes and unpacking though."

Donna smiles. "How 'bout this? I'll help you with the boxes, and Lucas can walk Abby down past the school. Show her around a little."

In the blink of an eye, both kids rubberneck to their mothers, speaking simultaneously.

"Can I, Mother?" asks Abby, over the moon.

"Do I have to?" asks Lucas, disgusted with the idea of being forced to hang out with a girl, and one he's only just met.

Karen wavers, briefly pondering her decision.

Donna continues. "I'll even make us some sweet tea. How's that sound?"

"You know what? That sounds like a great idea." Karen decides it may be best for her daughter to get to know the area and possibly make a new friend on day one, though it's obvious to everyone Lucas isn't on board with the idea.

"Whatever," Lucas says, shaking his head and sighing, once again disappointed with his mother's suggestion that he escape the confines of his home.

Donna's fed up. "Lucas Dean, you're gonna show this little girl around, and you're gonna be nice to her. And you're gonna stay out of trouble this time. Are you hearing me?"

"Yes, I hear you," Lucas says, accepting defeat and slumping his shoulders. "Come on," he says to Abby. He turns his back on her and heads off down the sidewalk without waiting, causing her to have to skip a few steps to catch up.

Abby, leaving her mother behind, gazes back at Karen and gives one last wave.

"Have fun!" Karen says.

"OK. We will," Abby says before she and Lucas continue into the distance.

CHAPTER 4

THE BULLIES

Lucas, still dismayed by his mother's offer to volunteer him to show some new girl around a school he isn't fond of, strolls down the sidewalk toward the school. Perky Abby lingers at his side, occasionally skipping a few steps to keep pace.

"How much farther?" She scans the area, taking in every bit of her journey to her new school.

Lucas, still unsure how to feel about Abby, continues forward without a response.

"My mom says I'll be able to make a lot of new friends here," Abby says, skipping a few more steps to keep stride with Lucas. "I think she's right. I haven't been here a whole day yet, and I already have one new friend. Exciting, huh?"

Lucas stops in his tracks.

Abby does the same.

"We're not friends," says Lucas.

"Why not? We're already going on our first walk together. We even have the same shoes and everything."

Lucas continues on, leaving Abby waiting for a reply.

"Well?" she asks.

"Well, you're probably a nerd. And I know you're a Goody Two-shoes."

Abby skips a few more steps to catch up.

"You don't know that. One time at my old house, me and my friend stayed up till almost three in the morning. And we didn't even eat dinner, just Moon Pies and Oreos. What do you think of that, huh?"

Wanting to laugh, Lucas holds back, letting only the slightest grin slip. He shakes his head at Abby's attempt to show how cool she can be.

"What's so funny, friend?" asks Abby.

The comment once again stops Lucas in his tracks. He's becoming more irritated and impatient with Abby.

"You really wanna be my friend?" he asks.

Abby eagerly nods, trying to hold back an enormous smile by biting her lower lip.

"Then start by not skipping anymore."

"So, if I stop, we can be friends?"

Lucas pauses for a moment, glaring at Abby and her overeager willingness to please.

"Whatever," he says. He rolls his eyes, and his head and rest of his body follow as he turns back down the sidewalk and continues on toward the school.

Behind Lucas's back, Abby gives a subtle celebration, letting her smile escape just before a stranger passing on the opposite side of the street catches her attention. Little by little, her smile fades. In her first moment of silence, Abby curiously ponders—her thought of her new friend gone for just a moment—as she watches the stranger walk on by.

Realizing Lucas has put some distance between them, Abby hightails it to catch back up, only to let her mouth take over where her feet had left off.

"How come your dad left you?" she asks, completely disregarding how inappropriate the question might be, especially with someone she's just met.

"He didn't leave me. He left my mom. He's coming back for me. He's probably waiting for the right time or something," Lucas says defensively.

"Your mom doesn't seem to think so."

"Yeah, well, my mom's the reason he left. Could you please stop talking?" Lucas is being pushed to his limit of personal questions.

"I can do that, especially for a friend," says Abby with pep.

Lucas lets his eyes shift to Abby, doubtful the silence will last.

"I know you don't think I can. But I can, anytime I want," Abby says.

Lucas's suspicions are confirmed.

Tired of Abby and her constantly running mouth, and with the school finally in sight, Lucas picks up the pace, hurrying ahead and leaving Abby and her questions behind.

"Hey, wait up," yells Abby, skipping a few steps to keep up.

Abby drags her hand along the chain-link fence as she and Lucas approach the old redbrick school. She sees blacktop basketball courts, grass fields, and a baseball diamond on the far back corner of the lot.

Lucas slows enough for Abby to keep pace without skipping as they make their way down the sidewalk to a gate, which is chained and pad-locked shut.

"This it?" Abby asks.

"Yeah, come on."

Pushing on the gate and adjusting the chain to create a large-enough gap to fit through, Lucas squeezes under the chain, through the gap, and onto the school grounds.

"Are we allowed to go through there?" Abby says, concerned about get-ting in trouble on her first day in town.

"I thought you weren't a Goody Two-shoes," Lucas says, playing off Abby's earlier proclamation of independence and willingness to break a few rules here and there.

He backs away from Abby with his hands up, letting her know the deci-sion is hers before he turns his back and heads off toward the school, leaving her behind.

Staring through the gate at Lucas, who's not hesitating in the slightest to move on without her, Abby pauses, questioning her morals while scanning the area for anyone who may see her about to commit this dubious act. After a brief moment of hesitation and fear, Abby breaks. Deciding to make a go of it, she squeezes through the gap and under the chain, willing to take the risk to make a new friend.

Lucas glances back over his shoulder to see Abby push herself through the gate and start skipping toward him.

Catching sight of Lucas watching, Abby transitions from a skip to a jog, not willing to risk the friendship over something so inconsequential, especially not after she's been willing to risk getting caught trespassing.

Now caught up and back at Lucas's side, Abby slows from a jog to a walk.

"I told you," Abby says, filled with pride.

"Told me what?"

"That I wasn't a Goody Two-shoes."

"Congratulations. You took the shortcut," Lucas says sarcastically.

Lucas points farther down the sidewalk at a gate purposely left open for pedestrians to gain access to the school yard.

"Oh," says Abby, disappointed her rebellious behavior was nothing but Lucas's unwillingness to walk another fifty feet down the sidewalk.

Lucas and Abby walk side by side, nearing the school and the point where the grass turns to blacktop. As they round a corner near the rear of the school and approach the basketball courts, two boys playing basketball come into view.

Lucas comes to a grinding halt.

He recognizes thirteen-year-old Daniel, who's a disrespectful bully, and his sidekick, twelve-year-old Jack, who's another ill-mannered delinquent. They're playing one-on-one basketball, though it looks more like an aggressive game of street ball, where rules and fouls don't apply.

"What's wrong?" asks Abby.

"Nothing. Let's just go."

Lucas changes direction in an attempt to escape without being seen, leaving Abby lingering on the blacktop, baffled.

"Where ya goin'?" Abby shouts.

The echo of Abby's call catches the boys' attention. They stop harassing each other for the moment and focus their efforts on another target.

Jack catches a glimpse of Lucas speed walking away around the corner of the school and grows a shit-eating grin as he watches Abby hurry after him.

Abby, trying to keep pace with Lucas, continually glances over her shoulder at the two bullies, who are staring her down like lions ready to pounce on an injured gazelle. Jack drops the ball and starts toward her and Lucas, motioning for Daniel to do the same. Daniel's and Jack's walks turn brisk and then into jogs. The boys want to make sure Lucas doesn't have the opportunity to escape without paying his toll.

As Daniel and Jack close in on Lucas and Abby, they slow their jogs into thuggish struts.

"Hey, Shit Stain!" says Jack.

Lucas tenses but continues forward, refusing to turn back and acknowledge Jack.

Abby, confused and out of place, remains unsure of what's about to unfold.

"Who's the bunny, Shit Stain?" asks Daniel.

Daniel closes in on Lucas and takes two quick steps. He lunges forward, shoving Lucas from behind and sending him stumbling forward. Lucas, able to steady himself before he hits the ground, regains his balance and turns back to confront his bullies.

Jack feeds off Daniel's comment. "Yeah. She's hot, but why's she with a fucking burnout?"

Daniel and Jack are now posted up in front of Abby and Lucas. Abby, although concerned for Lucas, doesn't seem scared for herself. Lucas, on the other hand, knows what's coming, as this isn't his first encounter with Daniel and Jack.

Daniel moves uncomfortably close to Lucas.

"Answer, Shit Stain! You fucking head case." He's closing the gap between himself and Lucas.

"I'm not a head case," Lucas says, still trying to defend himself without giving Daniel a reason to escalate the situation.

Wham!

Daniel's palms strike Lucas in the chest, knocking him to the ground. Lucas skins his elbows on the blacktop.

"Leave him alone!" Abby says. Panic stricken, she steps to Lucas and extends her hand, offering to help him from the ground. He denies her hand.

"Look, the bunny can talk," says Daniel.

Too proud to be helped by a girl, Lucas brushes Abby off and lifts himself from the ground. He rises and begins knocking the dirt off his clothes.

"Why are you hanging out with a burnout, Bunny?" Daniel asks Abby.

"I'm not a burnout," Lucas says, slightly raising his voice and standing his ground in an attempt to regain his dignity, even if it means taking another beating.

Annoyed by Lucas's willingness to defend himself, Daniel swiftly steps toward him, but not before Abby can throw herself between them.

Daniel and Abby now stand face to face, squared off to see who will break first. Tensions rise. Neither Abby nor Daniel seems willing to budge.

Jack chuckles. "Yeah, look at him. He's no burnout. He's just poor. A stupid, poor loser without a dad."

Daniel's stare finally breaks. He lets his eyes shift from Abby's and over her shoulder to Lucas. The bully is still seething and ready to kill.

"You had better leave him alone. Or else," says Abby, still in Daniel's face.

Daniel's eyes shift back to Abby's.

"Or else what? You gonna narc on us, Bunny?"

Abby relentlessly holds her position.

Daniel breaks again, this time cracking a smile at Abby, whose steadfast glare never wavers.

"Your bunny just saved you," he says to Lucas, keeping his eyes on the prize—that is, Abby.

Deciding to savor his moment with Lucas for another day, Daniel backs away with a smirk and a swagger.

"When you realize Shit Stain's a fucking loser, you make sure you come find me," he says with arrogance, causing Jack to chuckle.

Daniel, backing away and puckering his lips, blows a kiss to Abby before spinning around and heading back to the basketball courts, with Jack at his side. Unable to leave without expressing his feelings with one last gesture,

Daniel extends his middle finger to Abby and Lucas as he walks away, done with both of them—at least for today.

"Let's go home," says Lucas shamefully.

Sullenly he drifts back to the gate, embarrassed by his failure to defend himself and, even worse, by having had a girl do it for him.

Abby, still poised, continues to size up Jack and Daniel, who've since returned to their game of basketball. Her glare has turned to a slow burn.

Glancing back to Lucas, she realizes he's left the school yard and is on his way home without her.

"Hey, wait up!" she calls.

Abby sprints to the padlocked gate, squeezes her way under it, and races down the sidewalk to catch up with Lucas.

His hands in his pockets, Lucas trudges down the sidewalk. The heels of his beat-up Converse shoes scrape the ground with each overly oppressed step he forces himself to take. He doesn't know how much more bullying, or life in general, he can handle.

Abby catches up and slows her pace, still breathing heavily. Careful not to upset or embarrass Lucas any further, Abby decides it's best to say nothing for the moment. She wanders at his side, clutching her pendant.

After a few moments pass, when she and Lucas are nearly back home, Abby's no longer able to hold her tongue.

"If my dad were here, he would have made them sorry," she says.

"Well, he's not, and neither is mine, so drop it."

"Who were those guys?"

"Stupid jerks from my school."

"Why were they calling you—"

"Can we just drop it please? And what do you care anyway? All you did was make me look like a huge pussy."

"Sorry. I was just trying to help." Abby feels a bit guilty.

"You didn't."

"What can I do to help?" Abby hopes there's a way she can make this up to him.

"You can stay away from me."

Karen spots Abby and Lucas from her kitchen window as they walk down the sidewalk near their homes. She curiously watches the exchange.

Abby continues. "But I thought we were friends."

"We're not, and we never will be, so stop asking questions."

Having had enough of Abby and her questions and being close enough to home not to feel guilty about abandoning her Lucas surges ahead, leaving Abby by her lonesome on the sidewalk. He cuts across the neighbor's grass to his front door.

"Sorry!" Abby says.

Lucas's front door slams shut behind him.

Abby lowers her head. Overwhelmed and alone, she sluggishly shuffles to her front door and into the house.

It wasn't the start she had hoped for.

$$\blacktriangle$$

Karen, on edge, stands in the doorway between the living room and the kitchen, forcefully drying an already dry dish, ready to confront Abby as she enters.

The door creaks open, and Abby drags herself into the kitchen to her waiting mother.

"What was that, Abby?" asks Karen, continuing to dry the plate, nervous about Abby's dispute she was privy to witness.

Abby freezes like a deer in headlights. She wasn't expecting to see Karen awaiting her arrival.

"I thought I told you to make friends," Karen says.

"I was trying. I was super nice to him, but—"

"But what? We came here to get away from our problems, not create new ones."

"It's not like that." Abby's voice rises. "When we got up to the school, there were two boys picking on him. They kept calling him names, and one of them even pushed Lucas down."

Karen frowns as she stops drying the dish. She's worried about the reply she may receive from the question she's about to ask.

"And what did you do?"

"I didn't do anything. I asked them to stop, and when I tried to help, Lucas got all mad at me."

Karen sighs and extends her arms, pulling Abby in for a hug.

"I'm glad. It sounds like you did a good thing. Sometimes boys don't want help, especially from girls."

"Why?"

"It makes them feel insecure, like they can't take care of themselves."

"That's stupid."

"So are boys. So, you may as well get used to it." Karen shares a smile and a giggle with Abby. "I'm glad we're starting out on the right foot. Let's keep going down this path, and everything will work out."

"Thanks, Mommy."

With a warm smile, Abby reaches for her mother, hugging her once more.

CHAPTER 5

THE APOLOGY

Abby's bedroom is scattered with random personal belongings and boxes—some full, some half-unpacked. Her mattress lies on the ground, with the bed frame leaning against the wall rather than supporting the bed. They're the typical signs of the first night in a new home.

Abby, asleep on her mattress and covered by her comforter, begins to twitch. Her eyes flutter.

Tick. Tick. Tick.

Abby wakes. Her eyes heavily lift open as she rolls to her side, barely awake and unsure whether she's hearing the ticking or dreaming it.

Tick!

Abby's eyes flash open. The sound is real. In silence, she waits, listening closely for the sound to repeat.

Tick! Tick!

Leery, Abby rolls from her mattress and steps lightly to her window, patiently waiting for the noise to return.

Nothing.

Convinced the noise has gone, along with whatever was causing it, Abby reaches for her curtains to pull them open. Her fingers make contact with the fabric.

Tick!

Abby's body jolts, and she yanks her hand back. With a bold move and daring display of fearlessness, she snatches at the curtains and rips them open. To her surprise, all she finds is Lucas, hanging halfway out of his dimly lit window.

Abby, a bit puzzled about what Lucas could possibly want, especially at this hour, slides her window open and leans out.

"What are you doing?" she whispers.

"I felt bad about earlier."

"So you throw rocks at my window?"

"Beans."

"What?"

"I'm throwing beans." Lucas holds up a bag of dried beans, proud of his genius idea. "I figured it's a good way to make 'em disappear. It's that, or my mom makes me eat 'em."

Abby glances back at her clock.

"It's, like, one thirty in the morning. Couldn't this wait until tomorrow?"

"Probably. But I couldn't sleep, and I wanted to say sorry."

"That's it?"

Lucas shrugs, knowing he wants to say more but not wanting to come off as too eager. After all, he couldn't spoil his bad-boy image.

"Yeah. I guess so," he says.

"OK," Abby says, slightly cynical. "I'm going back to bed."

She begins to close her window.

"Hey, wait." Lucas tries to decide whether he should risk his image for a chance to make a new friend. He decides against it. "Never mind."

"Good night," says Abby.

She squints at Lucas, trying to figure him out, along with his true intentions. She places her hands back on her window and lowers it, giving him one last opportunity to spit out whatever's on his mind.

"Yeah. Night," Lucas says.

He throws his hand up for a quick wave, knowing he's missed an opportunity as he watches Abby's window shut and her curtains close.

Abby heads back to her bed. Arms at her sides, she lets her body flop onto the mattress. Lying facedown on her bed, she lets her eyes wander around her room before she rolls onto her back and stares at the ceiling, now wide awake and unable to help but wonder what Lucas wanted and what was holding him back.

A rustling noise from outside her window grabs her attention. She rises from her bed, tiptoes to her window, and places her hand between the curtains, opening them only enough to peek through.

She sees Lucas climbing down from his bedroom window and carefully closing it, mindful to be as quiet as possible before tiptoeing between the two houses and heading for the tree line of the forest behind their homes.

Abby follows him with her eyes, leaning against the window to see as much as she can before he's no longer in view. She lets her curtains close and backs away from the window, wondering what Lucas could possibly be up to, especially at this hour.

In a split-second decision, Abby scrambles around her room, quietly searching through the scattered mess until she finds her pair of black high-tops. She slips them on as fast as she can, just tucking the laces into the shoes, not bothering to tie them. Shoes on, she hops to her feet and hurries to her window. She pulls the curtains back, slides the window open, and crawls out.

Outside her window, Abby silently pulls it shut, making sure not to wake her mother. Abby glances toward the woods, no longer able to see Lucas, just the flicker of his flashlight reflecting off the trees. She sprints off in his direction, following what she's sure is him.

A few steps into the tree line, Abby begins to slow, carefully inching through some of the thicker brush as quietly as she can. Seeing the light up ahead, she pushes forward, still mindful of her every step, navigating past branches and other obstacles. It's getting harder to see as the forest thickens, becoming darker and denser the farther she treks.

As Abby closes in on Lucas, she pulls a small branch back and begins squeezing herself past it.

Snap!

The branch breaks. In the still of the night, the sound echoes like the crack of a .22 rifle's report, reverberating off every tree in the area.

Startled, Lucas spins around, shining his flashlight in the direction of the sound, searching for the culprit. He holds his position, afraid to move forward until he's satisfied he's alone and that only the sounds of the forest follow him.

As fast as Lucas turned, so did Abby, spinning herself back and ducking behind a tree, breathing lightly and making herself as skinny as possible. The light from Lucas's flashlight scrolls across the area where Abby just stood, past the tree she hides behind, and illuminates the area. Abby holds herself against the tree, frozen, hoping she hasn't been spotted as the light sweeps past once more.

Slowly but surely, the light moves on, brightening other sections of the forest. Abby sighs and lets the back of her head rest against the tree for a short time before she peeks to check the direction Lucas has headed. But she's in complete darkness.

The light is gone!

Alone in the darkness and worried, she blindly steps out from behind the tree. Putting one foot in front of the other, she heads in the direction she last saw Lucas. Barely able to distinguish the outlines of branches and fallen timber, she trips, and her body slams to the ground. She starts to panic. She jumps to her feet and presses forward with outstretched hands, her head swiveling, looking for a glimmer of light or any other signs of Lucas she can detect.

Staggering forward, she's less concerned about the noise and attention she may attract and more troubled by the reality she may not be able to find her way out until morning, if ever. Leaves, brush, and other forest debris crumble and crackle under her feet as she forges ahead.

Flash!

Light blinds Abby, causing her to freeze in her tracks. She emits a terror-stricken scream. The light drops from her eyes, and Lucas stands before her, rapidly throwing his hand over her mouth, hoping no one has heard the scream.

"What's your problem?" he whispers, letting his hand drop from her mouth.

"I don't have a problem. You're the one with the problem, waking me up in the middle of the night and sneaking off into the woods. And what are you doing out here anyway?"

"That's none of your business. Now go back."

"I'm not going back. I'm going with you."

"No, you're not! I don't need some Goody Two-shoes following me around through the woods, asking me questions all night long."

Abby takes a slow breath and holds her head high, letting her perky self shine through.

"OK. I'll go back," she says.

"Thank you."

"Straight back to your house to tell your mom you're out here."

Abby grins, turns, and takes a step in the direction of their homes.

"No, no, no, wait," says Lucas.

Abby spins back to Lucas with a manipulative smile.

"How's that for a Goody Two-shoes?" She's proud of her tactics.

"Whatever." Lucas is still annoyed with Abby, more for just being Abby than for any other reason. "If you're going with me, at least try to act cool. And you can't tell anyone we were out here. Ever!"

He turns away from Abby and back to his original path through the brush and trees. Abby jumps for joy and claps, excited Lucas has finally broken his resolve, even if just slightly, by letting her tag along. Her joyous celebration is cut short when he glances over his shoulder, causing her to stop. She doesn't want him to change his mind.

"I thought you were gonna be cool," Lucas says.

"Right. Cool."

Abby, unsure of what cool is or even how to pretend, draws finger pistols at Lucas, firing a few imaginary rounds.

"This is gonna be a long night," he says, marching on with Abby following in his footsteps.

⅄

Abby follows Lucas as they hike through the woods, all the while wondering what he's up to and where he's heading. Trying to keep from asking question after question, knowing it may prompt Lucas to head back home and abandon his evening altogether, she holds her tongue as long as she can before the floodgates open.

"So, where are you going anyway?" Her silence lasted barely more than five minutes.

"The old millpond."

"OK." Abby's mostly satisfied with his answer, as she'd be willing to follow him anywhere. "Wait, why?"

"What's with the questions? Do you wanna go or not?"

Sensing Lucas's growing frustration, Abby replies with only a nod and continues to follow him, trailing Lucas as he walks increasingly faster. He shakes his head at Abby's inability to keep quiet.

"Why are you always walking like you're trying to get away from me?" she asks.

"Questions." Lucas realizes the questions are never going to stop.

Sensing he's closing in on his destination, he starts walking faster and waves for Abby to keep up.

"Come on," he says, beginning to show signs of excitement.

"Are you sure you know where you're going?"

Ignoring Abby and her plethora of questions, Lucas ducks and dodges a few more trees as he scurries ahead. After pushing through a thicker section of brush, he rises, slowing to a stop, able to stand tall in the clearing.

Abby, still behind and trying to keep pace, pushes her way through the brush until she's made it to Lucas's side.

"What?" she asks, unsure why Lucas has stopped.

"We can take this all the way there," he says.

Lucas waves his flashlight down a wide dirt path separating the woods into two sections. The remnants of a railway have left only the path to the pond. A reminder of where the mill once operated.

"The train tracks used to go through here up until a couple of years ago. Since they've taken them out, no one really comes back here no more," says Lucas.

From the edge of the woods, Abby and Lucas step onto the dirt path and continue their journey side by side.

⁂

Lucas, no longer feeling the need to hurry or escape from Abby and all her questions, strolls the path with Abby at his side and his flashlight lighting the way.

"I guess this means we're friends now, huh?" asks Abby, with pep in her step.

"We'll see."

Abby smiles, hoping he's becoming open to the idea rather than denying her. But she'd be just as satisfied by him accepting they're going to be friends through the process of concession.

Pleased with this new development in their soon-to-be friendship, Abby skips a few steps but is quickly shut down as Lucas's head whips back toward her. He's still not used to or ready to accept the skipping or the consistency of her overly upbeat attitude.

"The night's not over yet," he says, skeptical Abby will be able to keep her spritely self in check.

Settling back into a walk and advancing farther down the path, Abby notices a glimmer of light flickering between the trees up ahead, just off to the side of the path.

"I thought you said no one comes out here anymore," she says.

"No one but Daniel and his dad. That's their cabin over there."

"Who's Daniel?"

"He's the one who kept calling you Bunny."

"Oh, right."

"The other one was Jack."

As the two draw near the cabin tucked back into the woods, just off the dirt path, Lucas stops, with Abby alongside him. Lucas reaches down and picks up a rock. He tosses it in the air a few times and catches it, never letting his eyes leave the cabin. He allows his hate for Daniel to build and considers smashing a window with that very rock. But he convinces himself doing so would come back to haunt him later, and it's not his lack of courage that holds him back.

Catching the stone one last time, Lucas holds it, takes a deep breath, and lets his shoulders slump forward. The rock slips from his fingers and joins others on the dirt path.

"After my dad left, Daniel's dad would come over and spend the night sometimes. I'm not sure exactly what happened, but after a while, he stopped showing up. That's when Daniel started acting like that," says Lucas, somber.

Abby's unsure of what to say that won't upset Lucas, so she gives him a moment to gather his thoughts. Lucas, his head down, focuses on one stone in particular. Still inside his own thoughts, he bends down, picks it up, and rotates it between his fingertips.

"He's stupid anyway," says Abby, hoping to cheer Lucas up and take him out of his funk.

Lucas looks up at her, gives a subtle half smile, and glances back at the rock before tossing it into the woods on the opposite side of the path. With nothing more to say, he continues on his way down the path to the old millpond.

Abby, however, waits, glaring back at the cabin for a moment before chasing after Lucas, not letting him get too far ahead.

⅄

At Lucas's side and with her arms crossed, Abby begins to shiver as the cool breeze of the Alabama backwoods flows down the path between the trees.

Lucas, mindful of the situation, unzips and removes his hoodie, extending it to Abby.

"Here," he says.

"Thanks." Abby blushes as Lucas holds the hoodie for her, and she slips her arms into the sleeves. Zipping the hoodie up and nervous to make eye contact with him, Abby is unable to control her heartfelt smile. As they continue their walk, Abby regains the courage to look at Lucas, wondering how long he'll continue to put on the tough-guy act.

"You don't have a lot of friends, do you?" she asks.

"What? I have friends. They don't live around here, so I don't get to see them a lot; that's all."

"OK. You know, I could be a pretty good friend."

"Give it a rest already. Hey, there it is."

Spotting their next obstacle ahead, Lucas dashes forward to an old train trestle that runs over a creek roughly twenty feet below. Abby jogs to keep up with him. She hears the increasing roar of the creek ahead as she approaches the trestle.

Standing in front of the trestle and beside Lucas, Abby stares down at the creek between the gaps of the old railroad ties. She lifts her head and looks to the other side of the trestle, able to detect the outline of the pond through the darkness.

"Let's go," says Lucas without hesitation.

"Are you sure it's safe?"

"I don't know. But a friend wouldn't let me cross it by myself." Lucas places his foot on the first railroad tie. He grins smugly, knowing good and well Abby would never pass up the opportunity to prove she could be a great friend to him.

Knowing she'll cross the trestle, Abby waits for a moment as she musters the courage. With Lucas now a few steps ahead, she places her first foot on the trestle, unable to ignore the gaps between the ties, allowing her to see exactly how far the drop is to the creek below. The way the creeks flows between the ties gives her slight vertigo, leaving her feeling woozy as she painstakingly places one foot in front of the other. She holds her arms out to balance herself.

Lucas, who's now on the other side, looks on with a delighted smile as Abby's confidence grows. She gradually increases her pace across the trestle. When she's nearly to the far side she places her foot on the last tie and looks up at Lucas with a sense of accomplishment. Maybe it's too soon.

As Abby attempts to take her last step, her foot catches the top of the last tie, and she drops to the ground. Though Abby's embarrassed she's tripped, she couldn't be more pleased she made it to the other side. Lucas helps her to her feet.

Back on her feet, Abby meets Lucas's gaze. Their eyes lock, and her heart pounds, about to beat out of her chest. The feeling travels north and manifests into a smile. It's contagious. Lucas smiles back and then begins to giggle, sparking Abby to do the same. She shares his laughter, even if it's at her own expense.

Their laughter spooks a deer in the nearby woods, sending it bolting across the path in front of them. Abby squeals but is muffled by Lucas, who throws his hand over her mouth.

"You're gonna get us caught," he whispers.

Lucas scans the area, listening to making sure Abby's scream hasn't drawn any unwanted attention. Satisfied they're in the clear, he smiles, triggering the return of the giggles.

"We'd probably better head back in case someone heard you," he says.

Abby nods and glances back at the trestle. Lucas extends his hand for hers—his first gesture of friendship. She places her hand in his, trying to control her breathing so as not to tip Lucas off about how nervous she is.

Leading the way, Lucas, with his hand in hers, escorts her across the trestle one step at a time, crossing with ease and with no unforeseen wild-animal adventures.

Flashlight bobbing in the night, Abby and Lucas spring from the woods and sprint to their homes. Abby's filled with a joy she had thought she left behind in California, along with her past. Abby and Lucas slow as they approach their homes and head back to their bedroom windows.

"Thank you," says Abby.

"For what?"

"It was fun."

"Yeah. I mean, I guess." Lucas reverts back to the tough-guy routine.

Abby turns to her window and places her hands on the sill, ready to hop through. But before she can, Lucas drops to a knee at her side. He interlocks his fingers and nods, offering to help. Abby, using his hands as a step, places her foot on his fingers and a hand on his shoulders. Lucas looks up, ready to hoist her, and their eyes meet once again. With a smile and a nod, he boosts her up and through the window.

"See you tomorrow," Abby says.

"OK. 'Bye." He rises from his knee.

Abby, knowing she's made a friend, waves to Lucas, feeling grateful for the new opportunities and the chance to leave her past where it lies—.

In the past.

Abby slides her window closed and shuts the curtains. She pulls her pendant from under her shirt and clutches it with both hands, grinning from ear to ear as she takes a step and throws herself on her bed. She lets out a playfully excited groan about the boy next door.

CHAPTER 6

A STRANGE ENCOUNTER

In the kitchen, Karen's busy unpacking boxes from the move. She sees Abby, who, in a zombielike trance and exhausted from lack of sleep, drags herself into the kitchen and slides herself into a chair at the table.

"You hungry?" asks Karen, continuing to unpack.

With a slow nod, Abby uses both hands to brush her hair back over her ears. Karen searches through a few of the many unpacked boxes scattered about the room until she finds a bowl and a spoon.

"Is there something I should know?" she asks, concerned by her daughter's lack of spritely energy. "You're not your perky self this morning. Seems like ever since your incident with that Lucas boy, you've been a little off. Should I be worried?"

Abby, still half-asleep, instantly lifts her head at the mention of Lucas's name.

"No, I promise. I'll make him a friend yet, just like you said. And he's really nice. I mean, he hasn't said we're friends yet, but I know he will." Abby slowly comes back to life.

Karen pours Captain Crunch cereal and milk into the bowl for Abby, who can see the hesitance to trust her quick judgment of Lucas in Karen's face.

"Really," Abby says. "I didn't get a lot of sleep last night because of the move and it being our first night here and all." She wants to ease her mother's concern.

"I see. Maybe the thought of some boy kept you up last night." Karen slides the bowl of cereal across the table to Abby, getting only a smile rather than an actual answer. "Either way, I'm glad you think you've found a friend already. Maybe this will help us get past all the things that happened back in California."

Karen's moment of hope and talk of moving forward with their lives is temporarily put on hold by the sound of the doorbell.

Karen goes to answer the front door, with curious Abby following behind. When Karen opens the door, she finds Donna standing on the doorstep, with Lucas tucked in behind her. Abby fears Donna's found out and that her and Lucas's days are numbered before they've even started.

"This might be a silly question, but I was makin' some chili for tonight, and I was wonderin' if y'all had some beans. I swear I bought some the last time I was at the store, but I can't find 'em," says Donna.

Relieved and amused, Abby leans out from behind her mother and gives Lucas a quick wave and a smile. In typical Lucas fashion, with zero emotion, he lifts his hand to say hello and steps behind Donna.

"To be honest, I have no idea," Karen says. "Even if I did, I don't know if I'd be able to find them. The house has been such a mess, with the move and all."

"That's OK. I guess I was hoping not to go into town is all. Oh well. Tell you what—how 'bout when it's done, I bring you a bowl?"

"You've been so kind; thank you."

"All right then. If you find yourself wantin' to take a break, you're more than welcome to stop by."

"See, there you go being nice again, but I really do have so much to catch up on."

"I understand. Suppose I better get goin'. I'll stop by later when it's all finished."

"I'm looking forward to it. 'Bye."

"'Bye, honey."

Abby peeks past her mother for one last glimpse of Lucas before Karen closes the door, and she catches a brief moment of him leaking a smile before he lets his normal annoyed-with-the-world-and-everyone-in-it glare take over. The smile is infectious, lighting Abby's face as the door closes.

⋏

From the empty aisle of a grocery store, the sound of a repetitive squeaky wheel escalates until Donna, with an unlit cigarette dangling from her mouth, turns the corner. One of the front wheels on her cart spins erratically, occasionally reversing direction as it skips off the ground.

Lucas, who'd rather be any place other than following his mother through the grocery store, trails behind, poking at items on the shelves, knocking them back from what was a neatly faced aisle, and doing anything he can to alleviate the boredom.

Donna stops and pulls a box of flavored rice from the shelf and begins reading it, not for the nutritional value but for the cooking time. She's already found herself behind in the day by having to go to town for beans she's sure she'd already bought in the first place.

Slap!

The sound breaksDonna's concentration and her head whips back toward Lucas. He stands with a dumbfounded expression and a box on the floor in front of him. Rather than picking up the box and placing it back on the shelf from which it fell, Lucas glares, locked in a standoff with his mother.

Bothered not just by Lucas testing to see exactly how far he can push her but also by the fact she's been inconvenienced by a child interfering with her life since day one, Donna drops the rice into the cart, throws a hand onto her hip, and leaves the box on the floor.

Deciding he may have pushed her as close as he can to her breaking point, Lucas picks up the box and places it back on the shelf, though he makes sure not to place it back how it belongs.

Donna's done playing. "Now why don't you make yourself useful for a change and go get some damn milk." She's doing all she can to hold back from exploding at Lucas.

Sulking about losing another battle with his mother, Lucas scowls as he leaves the aisle in search of a gallon of milk. Before he leaves the aisle, he glances back at her; she's pushing her cart and browsing a few of the items as she passes. Noticing this is his chance to get in one last jab without repercussion, he reaches out and knocks another item off the endcap as he turns the corner.

Bang!

Donna spins around, ready to let Lucas have it, but she finds only a box of crackers lying on the floor.

⤵

Lucas, carrying a gallon of milk, peers down every aisle in search of his mother. When he finds her, he pauses at the end of the aisle. He slumps his shoulders and rolls his eyes at the sight of her flirting with the thirty-five-year-old sheriff's deputy, Alex Morgan.

As Lucas apprehensively approaches his mother and Deputy Morgan, he knows that even though she was ignoring him just moments ago, he's about to become nonexistent. Donna has only one real concern in her life: men.

"So, like I said, tonight I'm making chili, but tomorrow night maybe I can make something for you," she says to Deputy Morgan in a sensual voice, letting her finger float down the buttons of his shirt and giving a tug at one of them.

Deputy Morgan, enjoying every second of Donna's supermarket seduction, wears a slick smile as he closes in on her.

Slam!

Donna and the deputy recoil and back away from each other. The deputy's smile is wiped away by the crashing sound of Lucas dropping the milk into the cart.

"Goddamn it, Lucas. Now look at what you did," says Donna.

Lucas, in an attempt to break up his mother's current public display of provocativeness, had dropped the milk into the cart and directly on the bread, flattening it. Donna pulls the bread from the cart and shoves it into his chest.

"Now go grab a new one!"

Lucas stands motionless, staring at the deputy.

"Well, go," says Donna, reaching her limit with Lucas.

Taking a few steps back, with his eyes still glued on the deputy, Lucas turns away, storms down the aisle, and rounds the corner, leaving Donna to her duties with the deputy.

Nearly at his breaking point with his mother and her willingness to discard her only son at the drop of a hat for any Tarzan who swings her way, Lucas wanders down the bread aisle, barely keeping his temper in check as he searches for the loaf of bread he's smashed, which he doesn't care to eat to begin with.

Standing in front of the bread, scanning the different brands, he spots an identical loaf—albeit not smashed—pulls it from the shelf, and tucks the smashed loaf in its place. As he releases his hand from the destroyed loaf of bread, he pauses for a moment, appreciating how that particular loaf stands alone among the others.

Even though it's different from all the others, a smashed loaf of bread is still a loaf of bread.

Lucas's appreciation for the unique transforms to bitterness. He lashes out in a fit of rage, smashing loaf after loaf until a stranger turning his cart into the aisle catches him by surprise. Lucas stops the destruction of conformity and hurries from the aisle before being pegged as the culprit.

The stranger catches a glimpse of Lucas rounding the corner. He becomes curious about Lucas and glances down the aisle in the direction he fled, noticing the multiple loaves of smashed bread.

Riding a high from his momentary release, Lucas is unable to find his mother in any of the aisles. He walks to the front of the store and spots her in one of the checkout lanes, unloading her cart onto the conveyor. The young gum-smacking cashier, who seems unable to care less whether she works there or not, keys in the prices one item at a time and at her own pace.

Lucas steps up behind his mother and tosses the bread on the conveyor just as she lifts the milk from the cart to the conveyor, nearly smashing another loaf. Donna, without a word, glances back at Lucas, letting him know he's avoided a punishment by only inches.

"Your total comes to twenty seventy-nine," says the cashier.

Donna digs through her purse, removes a twenty-dollar bill, hands it to the cashier, and returns to her purse to look for exact change.

The irritated cashier lets her head fall to one side and lifts her eyes while staring at Donna. She smacks her gum just loudly enough to let Donna know that the cashier and the rest of the customers in line are waiting because of Donna's inability to count to seventy-nine fast enough.

Donna pulls the change from her purse and begins to hand it over to the cashier but drops a dime in the process. The cashier rolls her eyes. The dime hits the ground, rolls, and stops against the foot of the man behind Donna. He reaches down, picks up the dime, and hands it over to her, and she smiles flirtatiously.

Lucas recognizes the man is the same one from the bread aisle and stares at him. Other than the near miss with the bread, Lucas thinks he's seen him before. It's a small town with few unfamiliar faces, just those who haven't introduced themselves yet.

Donna can't stop flirting. "Thank you so much. Nice and good lookin', well, how 'bout that?"

The stranger cracks a slight smile that fades quickly as he turns to Lucas, whose stare continues.

Smacking the back of Lucas's head, Donna brings him back into the moment, instantly fixing his staring problem.

"I'm sorry, Good Lookin'. My son here seems to have a staring problem today."

"Ma'am," says the cashier, tapping her freshly manicured nails against the register, waiting for Donna to finish her transaction.

"Oh, right."

Donna hands the coins over to the cashier, finishing her transaction and satisfying the cashier's newfound sense of urgency. Donna takes her receipt and pushes her cart from the checkout lane toward the door, stopping to tuck her receipt into her purse. Not overlooking one last opportunity to flirt, she turns back to the stranger and shoots him a wink.

"Thanks again, Shugga."

"Mom, let's just go," says Lucas, having had enough embarrassment from his mother's promiscuity for one day.

Donna snatches Lucas by his arm, pulls him in close, and quietly threatens him through her teeth.

"You need to watch how you talk to me," she says.

With her grip digging into his arm, she pulls him in tighter and keeps his body right up against hers. She forces him from the store with one hand and pushes the cart with the other.

The stranger takes special interest as he watches Donna drag Lucas from the store.

CHAPTER 7

WITH THIS KISS

Awake in her bed, Abby lies fully dressed, eagerly waiting and hoping for another midnight run with Lucas. She rolls to her side and glances at the clock on her dresser: 11:13 p.m. Growing impatient, she tosses herself off the bed, hops to her feet, and moves to her window. Peeking through the curtains at Lucas's window across the way, she sees nothing but closed blinds.

Disappointed, Abby drags herself back to her bed and collapses on her mattress, wondering whether the moment she shared with Lucas the night before was but a dream. Was it really there? Did Lucas feel it too, or was she so eager to find a friend that she manifested the whole thing? All she can do now is wonder.

She's facedown in her bed, and her eyelids begin to flutter as she awakens. Through the drowsiness, a blurred time of 1:21 a.m. shows on her clock but fades from sight as the weight of her eyelids becomes too much to overcome. They close, but just as fast, they flash open, and Abby springs to an upright position, directing her attention to her window.

She scoots off the edge of her mattress and rushes back to the curtains to take another glance across the way at Lucas's room. Unfortunately, Lucas's blinds are still closed, with no light behind them. Abby's mind begins to race, worrying the feelings weren't mutual but manifested by her own desires. She lets her curtains close and posture slump as sorrow sets in.

With her head down in front of her window, Abby looks at her bedroom door. She's done wondering. Rather than wait, she's about to find out.

She hurries through her bedroom door, down the hall, and into the kitchen. Quickly but quietly, she rummages through one of the cabinets. Finding what she was looking for, she closes the cabinet and races down the hall and back to her room with a bag in one hand.

Back in her room, she gingerly shuts the door behind herself and heads straight to her window. She opens the curtains, slides her window open, and leans halfway out. She reaches into the bag, pulls something out, and throws it at Lucas's window.

Tick!

Before Abby can reach back into her bag and grab another pea, a light flickers in Lucas's room. He draws his blinds and pulls his window open.

"Hey," Lucas says, acknowledging the bag in Abby's hand.

"You wanna go hang out again?" she asks, about to find out either way whether the feeling of friendship was mutual or a manifestation.

"I mean, I guess we could," he says.

It clearly is not the obvious one-sided answer Abby was hoping for, but it's definitely better than a solid no, so she'll take it. And the smile on her face shows it.

Lucas climbs down from his window fully dressed, with his flashlight in hand.

"Whatcha throwin'?" he asks, extending his hand to Abby to help her from her window.

"Peas," she says, placing her hand in his.

"Good one."

"Wait. Were you waiting for me?" She pulls her hand back, realizing how quickly Lucas had hopped out of his window, ready to go upon request.

"What? No," he says, trying to play it cool.

"Then how come you have all your clothes on?"

"Do you want help out or not?"

"Yeah. As soon as you admit you were waiting for me." Abby knows the answer but wants to hear it from him.

Lucas calls Abby's bluff and turns back to his house. He takes only two steps before Abby folds.

"OK, OK. Just help me out," she says, giving in to Lucas's stubbornness.

Lucas turns back, extends his hand, and helps Abby down from her window. The two share a quick smile and break for the tree line. Side by side, they run. Abby, glancing over at Lucas, feels as if she's floating free of the world and her problems, keeping them in the past along with the rest of the world as she and what may be her first real friend live in the moment.

⋏

Abby and Lucas travel down the old dirt path past Daniel's cabin and approach the old train trestle. They stop before crossing and look between the ties at the creek below. Lucas, with his eyes ahead, turns his palm up at his side, extending his hand to Abby. She catches a glimpse of the creek and then looks up at him. Not wanting to stare, she leans out over the trestle and places her hand in his. Lucas takes the first step, helping guide her across.

"Watch that last step; it's loose," he says with a grin, taking a quick jab at Abby for tripping over it the night before.

"I remember. Thanks," she says sarcastically.

"Here, let me help."

Lucas holds her hand firmly and helps her across the last railroad tie on the trestle. Though that tie is no different from any of the others and presents no real danger, Lucas's gesture to Abby shows he's genuinely concerned about her safety and considerate enough to be thinking of her, despite his too-cool-for-school attitude.

With their feet back on the ground on the far side of the trestle, Abby and Lucas beam with delight, relieved they've made it across without incident. Abby lowers her head, and her eyes wander to her hand in his, drawing his eyes there as well. They lift their heads and meet each others' eyes. Lucas, unfamiliar with the feeling and unsure of himself, awkwardly pulls his hand from Abby's.

"Be careful a deer doesn't get you again," he says in an attempt to use humor to break the tension.

"Ha-ha."

"Over here," Lucas says.

Excited they've made it but even more so to show Abby his secret spot, he takes off toward the pond.

⨘

Most of the pond is surrounded by tall grass, with the exception of a small gravel beach that opens near the water. Lucas leads the way to the clearing, with Abby following closely behind. Near the water, Abby and Lucas find a spot that's less rocky than the rest and plant themselves down, brushing away a few of the bigger rocks. Unwinding in the tranquility of the peaceful night, Abby and Lucas both sit in the silence, unsure of the next move.

"It's peaceful here," says Abby, trying to spark any form of conversation.

Lucas nods as he searches through the gravel, brushing a few more stones away.

"Do you come here a lot?" Abby asks.

"Only since my dad left. Sometimes I don't wanna be home no more, so I come down here, usually at night when it's quiet like this." Lucas sounds sad as he thinks about how he sneaks out to get away from the noises made by his mother and her man of the month. Lucas plucks a stone from the gravel and tosses it into the pond.

"I feel like that sometimes. But I don't have a place like this to go to, so I close my eyes and remember that my dad is always with me, no matter where I am."

Abby, out of habit alone, pulls out the pendant that hangs from her neck and clutches it, watching Lucas as he tosses another rock into the pond. A pebble between her and Lucas catches her eye. She reaches for it and, like her friend Lucas, chucks it into the pond.

"Good throw," says Lucas. Abby couldn't be more pleased to receive a compliment from him. He continues, "Now that you live here, you can... uh...you can always come down here. You know, so you have a place to go and all."

47

"It's nice to have somewhere to go." Abby pulls her knees to her chest. "Especially with a friend." She subtly tries to get Lucas to jump onboard with the whole friend thing.

He doesn't reply, but his blushing face reveals his feelings.

Abby sifts through the rocks, building her courage to reask the next question.

"You don't really have a lot of friends, do you?"

Lucas lowers his head. His fingers fidget through the stones.

"It's OK," Abby says. "I never really had any friends either. You're actually my first real friend."

Not wanting to push Lucas too far, Abby decides it's best to ease off on the questions and let things simmer for a bit. She reaches for another stone between herself and Lucas, but his hand is still sweeping the gravel, and Abby places her hand directly on his. Hearts pounding, both kids quickly pull away.

"Sorry. You take it," says Lucas, letting his eyes wander everywhere but directly at Abby.

"No, you."

He smiles, avoiding eye contact, still unsure of how to deal with his feelings for her. He picks up the stone and rolls it through his fingers a few times before skipping it across the pond. The splash breaks the uncomfortable silence.

Abby stares out at the tiny waves thinking about how even the smallest stone cast on the largest pond can have rippling effects.

As Lucas's courage progressively builds, he gathers his words and turns to Abby.

"So, does this mean you've never had a boyfriend either?"

Speechless and blushing, Abby shakes her head and smiles. Lucas, still timid and skittish, draws in the dirt with his finger, contemplating whether or not he's bold enough to ask the next question.

"What if, maybe, I was your boyfriend?"

"Yeah," she says in nothing more than a whisper. She shrugs and bites her lower lip.

Lucas, still doing what he can to avoid eye contact, gives a subtle nod and fidgets, unsure what to do with his hands. With her head down, Abby scoots herself close enough to him that her body rests against his. She too begins to fidget with her fingers in her lap, unsure where to place them.

"Does this mean we have to kiss each other?" she asks, ignorant of the boyfriend-girlfriend formalities.

"I don't know." Lucas shrugs, afraid to say yes.

Abby repositions herself, turning ever so slowly toward Lucas. With his heart ready to explode, he turns to her and lifts his head. Abby and Lucas lean in, pressing their lips against each others'. Then, breathing uncontrollably, they pull away, staring deep into each others' eyes.

With a deep breath, Abby settles back into her spot, tucking her knees back under her chin. Filled with emotions she's never felt before, she begins to tremble lightly.

"Are you cold?" asks Lucas.

"No, I just…I'm fine." Abby blushes as she brushes the hair over her ear. "So, now what?"

Still bashful, Lucas grabs another rock. But just before he pulls back to toss it, he brings it back in, glares at it, and rolls it through his fingers. An idea strikes him, and he raises his head toward Abby.

"We should do something that proves we really like each other. You know, since we're boyfriend and girlfriend and all," Lucas says with new confidence.

"We did just kiss."

"No, I didn't mean—"

"I know," Abby says, having returned to her perky self.

She reaches for her pendant and removes it from her neck. She takes Lucas by the hand and places her pendant in it. Lucas, unsure of what to say, stares at it and then back up at Abby.

"I want you to have this. But you have to wear it," says Abby.

"OK. But that's not exactly what I meant."

"You have to promise me that you'll wear it, though. It'll keep you safe."

"Keep me safe from what?"

"Just promise!"

"OK, I promise."

Lucas slips the necklace over his head, giving the trinity-shaped pendant a once-over before slipping it into his shirt.

"When my dad gave me that necklace, that's what he told me. He said it would remind me that he'd always be there to keep me safe. Now it can remind you that I'll always be there for you, just like he is for me."

"But what's gonna keep you safe?" Lucas asks.

"You, silly," Abby says with a playful grin.

Lucas smiles back. With his confidence grown, he pulls the pendant back out to take another look, and his eyes shift to the rock in his other hand. He springs to his feet and reaches for Abby's hand to help her up, ready to take a chance at this once-in-a-lifetime opportunity.

"Let's go see if it works," Lucas says, filled with a vigor that had been buried deep until now.

"What?"

"Let's go."

Reluctant and confused, Abby follows Lucas anyway as he hurries back up toward the trestle, waving for her follow.

⅄

Lucas races down the dirt path, half dragging Abby behind him. They slow as they approach a light in the distance. It's Daniel's cabin. Lucas turns back to Abby and presses his index finger to his lips, signaling for her to keep quiet as they move closer.

"What are we doing?" she whispers, letting her hand slip from Lucas's.

Lucas glances back and shushes her as he continues to creep forward, getting a better view of Daniel's cabin. Now with the cabin in plain view, Lucas begins searching the dirt path as if he's lost something. At last, he picks up a stone.

"Ready?" he asks.

"Ready for what?"

Lucas grins like a villain. He takes a step back from Abby, spins toward the cabin, and hurls the rock as hard as he can. Abby's eyes widen as the rock floats through the air toward the cabin, with Lucas's arm reached out after his follow-through.

Crack!

The rock bounces off the roof and rolls back to the ground. Abby and Lucas scramble, throwing themselves into the trees and brush in front of the cabin, waiting for movement, making sure it's safe to move without being seen.

They look at each other, satisfied they're in the clear. Their wariness turns into laughter and gets progressively worse as they shush each other, causing them to laugh hysterical while attempting to be as quietly as possible. Gradually, the laughter fades, and Abby and Lucas are able to gather themselves

"Now you go," Lucas says. "We're in it together. Boyfriend and girlfriend, right?"

Abby wavers for a moment before giving Lucas a nod.

"OK," she says.

Rising to a knee, she takes the ponytail holder from around her wrist and throws her hair up into a ponytail and out of the way. Hair up, she gets to her feet and scans the area for a stone, finding the perfect specimen She picks up the stone and glances at Lucas, who nods. Abby plants her feet, closes her eyes, and flings the rock, sending it flying through the air toward the cabin.

Crash!

The rock smashes through a window, shattering glass everywhere. Abby's hands immediately cover her mouth as she stares in awe at what she's done. Lucas jumps to his feet and grabs Abby by the arm in an attempt to coax her to flee the scene, but she doesn't budge. A light inside the cabin flashes on.

"Abby, let's go," Lucas says, trying to get her attention, knowing they're about to get caught.

A voice from the cabin brings Lucas to a standstill. Abby snaps back to reality as they turn to each other and then back toward the cabin.

"What the fuck?" the voice says.

"Go, go, go!" Lucas panics as they sprint off through the forest.

The door to the cabin slams open. Daniel's father, Dale Stetson, who's in his late forties and wearing only pajama bottoms, bursts out. He's wielding an old double-barrel shotgun and scanning the area for the trespasser. Pointing his gun into the sky, he fires a round, hoping to spook anyone who may still be hiding in the area into giving him- or herself up.

Never slowing their pace through the woods, dodging tree limbs and brush, Lucas and Abby dip at the sound of the gunfire, now having even more motivation to push themselves.

Still on his porch, staring out at the night, Mr. Stetson continues to scan the area.

"Who the fuck's out there? Show yourself, you piece-of-shit hoodlums!"

He takes a few steps into the darkness for a better look yet finds nothing but the night. Behind him, Daniel steps into the doorway in his pajamas, looking out at his father.

"Get back in the house," Mr. Stetson says, cautiously backing into his doorway and posting up, not yet ready to quit in case the guilty party is a few feet away in the dark and about to make the mistake of showing him- or herself.

Flashlights flicker off the tree line at the edge of the woods behind Abby's and Lucas's homes as they flee. The run from their recent mischief and near-death experience has left them winded and worn out, slowing them to a walk as they approach the space between their bedroom windows.

Tossing her hands onto her hips, Abby takes a few deep breaths, trying to replenish her lungs. She looks over at Lucas, who's bent over with both hands on his knees, the pendant dangling from around his neck. He peeks back up at Abby, grinning, with a feeling of liberation and consummation.

"I can't believe you broke his window," he says, still sucking wind.

"Me neither." Abby chuckles. "I was aiming for the roof."

Rejoicing in their narrow escape, Abby and Lucas share a laugh.

"We'd better get back in," Lucas says.

"Yeah."

"Here, I'll help."

Lucas once again drops to a knee, cups his hands, and allows Abby to step up and through her window.

"Tomorrow?" Abby asks.

"Yeah. Night."

Abby, filled with joy, looks on as Lucas runs to his window, slides it open, and effortlessly flings himself through. Abby slides her window shut, pulls the curtains, and heads back toward her bed. As she reaches for her covers, her bedroom door swings open.

Karen drifts into the doorway.

Speechless, Abby leaves her covers for the moment and rises, fearful of her punishment. Surely her mother knows she's been gone. In the doorway with her arms crossed, Karen gives Abby a once-over.

"What are you doing?" Karen asks.

"I thought I heard something outside," Abby says, trying to drum up anything that may seem like a reasonable explanation for her misbehavior.

"Why are you dressed?"

Unable to think of a reasonable explanation off the top of her head, Abby chooses to stay silent rather than dig herself into a deeper hole.

"I can't do this again, Abby," Karen says with a hint of sorrow in her voice.

Abby's fear of punishment changes to anger and resentment within seconds, her posture shifting slightly to the offensive.

"Then don't," Abby says, waiting to see whether Karen's going to draw the courage to make the next move. "You need to leave my room, Mother!"

Karen stands her ground.

Abby's fists and teeth begin to clench. Her breathing becomes heavy and laborious, and her nostrils flare with every breath.

"I said get the fuck out!"

Karen, saddened by the resurgence of a behavior she hoped had been left behind in California, shudders at the thought that it may be returning. Indecisive, Karen steps back out into the hallway and closes the door behind herself.

Infuriated beyond her own control, Abby glares at the door as it latches shut.

CHAPTER 8

Play Ball

The living room of Abby's house is eerily quiet except for the ticking of the wall clock.

When the doorbell rings, she darts out of her bedroom door and down the hallway to the front door.

"I got it!"

She pulls the front door open and finds Lucas standing on the porch, with a wooden Louisville Slugger resting over his shoulder.

"You wanna hang?" he asks.

"Yeah. I'll be out in a sec."

Abby closes the door, hurries to the couch, and plops down. She snatches her black Converse shoes from the floor, throws them onto her feet, and ties them as fast as she can, not wanting to waste any time she could be spending with Lucas.

"Mom, I'm leaving," she yells.

"Where do you think you're going, Abby?" Karen asks from another room.

"Outside with Lucas!"

"Abby, you're not going."

Abby stops tying her shoe. Irked by her mother's attempt at parenting her, she lifts her head toward the hallway, where her mother's voice had echoed, and then lets it fall back to her shoe. She finishes tying it and rises from her seat.

"I'm going outside with Lucas, Mother," Abby yells, being very blunt and direct.

Skittish and stressed out, Karen warily lingers near the border of the hallway and the living room. Unsure of herself and her control over Abby, she decides to make a bold attempt at showing her daughter she's not intimidated, though her face and body language say otherwise.

"Abby, I am your mother, and you're going to listen to me," Karen says hesitantly.

Abby rises from the couch. "Or what? You do remember what happened last time, don't you, Mother?" Abby asks fiercely.

Placing her hand over the scar on her neck and lightly stroking it, Karen thinks back to a time she'd hoped to forget.

Abby continues, "Now I'm gonna tell you again. I'm going outside with Lucas, Mother."

Abby's glare slowly burns, digging deep into Karen's thoughts. Deciding she's made herself clear, Abby heads to the front door. Placing her hand on the doorknob she begins to look back over her shoulder but stops, deciding against it. She exits and slams the door behind herself instead.

Left standing in the hallway, Karen exhales deeply, hanging her head in defeat.

Waiting for Abby out in front of her house, Lucas scrapes the end of his bat against the sidewalk, wondering what's taking her so long. Just then, Abby pops out of her front door, slamming it but letting the screen door close on its own, seemingly without a care in the world.

"So, where we going?" she asks as she approaches Lucas.

"Anywhere but here." He leads the way down the sidewalk.

"Your mom again?"

"How'd you guess?" Lucas isn't surprised Abby was able to figure out that incomprehensible mystery. "I don't even know what I did this time. I kinda want to run away."

Unsure how to respond to what is surely something Lucas has actually considered as an option, Abby perks up, wanting to change the current mood of their adventure. She backpedals in front of him.

"Let's race," she says, trying to entice him, but he would rather continue at his own pace. "Come on." Lucas doesn't bite. "Chicken."

Still not getting a response from Lucas, who's now clearly annoyed, Abby slumps her shoulders and falls back in line next to him.

Lucas sprints away.

"First one to the gate wins!" he hollers, leaving Abby unexpectedly behind.

"Cheater!"

Abby sprints after him, trying to keep up as they approach the gate to the school grounds. But his lead is too great for her to overcome. Lucas wins the race and grabs the gate, holding himself up as he catches his breath. Abby jogs up behind him, grinning from ear to ear, even after losing to him and his dirty tactics.

"Totally beat you," says Lucas.

"Totally cheated."

Spirits high, Lucas squeezes through the gate under the lock and then turns back to push the gate apart from the fence, at least as far as the chain holding them together will allow, making it easier for Abby to do the same.

Lucas and Abby go through the gate and head toward the school, but Lucas stops upon seeing Daniel and Jack back out on the basketball courts.

"Let's go over here," Lucas says, pointing toward the baseball diamond with his bat and hoping to avoid the two bullies. He grabs Abby by the hand and leads her toward the dugout. Willing to follow Lucas anywhere, she does, though her icy stare back at Daniel and Jack says she's not ready to concede the school's grounds as easily as Lucas does.

"Why don't you just stand up to them?" she asks as Lucas leads her into the dugout. They sit down on the benches.

"Easy for you to say. They aren't gonna beat up a girl. Besides, even if I did, I'd get in even more trouble with my mom." Lucas rubs his bat through the sand and shelled sunflower seeds that litter the dugout floor, wondering whether there's anything he'll ever be able to do to satisfy anyone. "It doesn't matter what I do anyway. I always end up being wrong. Someday I'll be gone, and then she'll be sorry."

Lucas slumps back against the cinderblock wall, still stirring the dirt between his legs with his bat.

"What about me?" Abby asks.

"You could come with me."

Brushing her hair over her ear, Abby grins at the thought of her and Lucas running away together, just the two of them. No rules, no bullies, and no overbearing mothers.

"Where would you go?" Abby asks.

"Anywhere's better than here."

"You know, my dad—"

"Hey, Bunny," Daniel says.

The bully pops his head into the dugout. He then strolls the rest of the way in.

"What do you want, Daniel?" Lucas asks.

"I just want to talk. That's all."

Lucas rises to his feet and grips Abby's hand, giving her a tug, implying she should rise. On their feet, Abby and Lucas back away as Daniel continues a methodical march forward, closing in on them, clearly intending to prove he's the alpha male.

Daniel is blocking one of the entrances, and Abby and Lucas continue toward the other until Jack slides into view, blocking the only other exit.

"Where do you think you're going, Shit Stain?" asks Jack, lurking around the corner of the dugout.

"Leave us alone, jerk," says Abby.

"Your bunny isn't gonna save you this time," says Daniel.

Head swiveling, Lucas glances back and forth between Daniel and Jack as they close in, and he pulls Abby in close behind him. Jack makes the first move, taking a step forward and reaching for Abby. Without hesitation, Lucas spins back and swings his bat, landing a blow right to Jack's midsection, knocking the wind out of him and dropping him instantly. Simultaneously, Abby jumps forward and swiftly kicks Daniel straight in the groin, sending him into the dirt.

With both Daniel and Jack temporarily out of commission, Lucas snatches Abby by her shirt, yanking her from the dugout, scrambling to escape before the two bullies regain their ability to retaliate.

"You're fucking dead, Shit Stain," yells Daniel, still buckled over in pain.

Moments later, he rises to a knee. Fire burns in his eyes as he watches Abby and Lucas run from the school grounds and off into the distance, while Jack tries to regain his breath.

⊼

Slowing from their sprint, Abby places her hands on her hips. Lucas, holding each end of his bat across his shoulders, sucks oxygen into his lungs as he and Abby gather themselves and share smiles of accomplishment as they approach their homes.

Karen, dusting her blinds in the front window inside her house, notices Abby and Lucas drawing near. Curious to see how Abby's interaction with Lucas compares to what she's been told by her daughter, Karen secretly keeps an eye on the two children as she continues to clean.

"That was crazy. I can't believe you did that," Lucas says, still out of breath but filled with pride and accomplishment, having stood up to his bullies for the first time.

"He deserved it. And me? You totally hit Jack so hard. I'm pretty sure he started crying." Abby's adrenaline is still surging through her veins, and her stomach is still turning from the butterflies.

"I'm really glad you moved here," Lucas says.

"Me too," Abby says, glowing.

"I meant what I said about running away."

"I know."

In a brief moment of silence, Lucas reaches for Abby's hand. Placing her hand in his, Abby takes a step forward. Closing in and rising to her tiptoes, she leans in for a kiss.

"Abby!" Karen yells, nervously watching her and Lucas nearly kiss, stopping them in the nick of time. "Can you come here please?"

Irritated, Abby settles back onto her feet without the kiss.

"I have to go," she says.

Left hanging, Lucas nervously fidgets. Should he lean in for another attempt or let it be until next time?

"OK," he says, deciding to wait.

Karen yells once again. "Abby?"

"I'm coming! God!" Abby yells back toward the house, annoyed by her mother's persistence. "'Bye," she says to Lucas.

"See ya."

Abby reluctantly lets Lucas's hand slip from hers as she pulls away. She walks back to her house, knowing after today's chain of events she's bound to be bonded to Lucas for life, whether he's prepared for it or not. An unprepared and unknowing Lucas has no idea what he's in for as he watches with pure joy as Abby, with a hop and a skip, heads off into her house, letting the door slam behind her.

Abby pops through the front door, looks for her mother, and finds her cleaning the blinds in the front window of the living room.

"Yeah?" asks Abby, waiting to see what was so important she had to stop what she was doing to help.

"Oh, can you…uh…hand me that rag please?" Karen asks.

"That's what you called me in here for?"

Abby looks over at the window and takes a few steps closer, curious why her mother couldn't reach down for the rag herself. Then she spots it. Through the window, Abby gets a good look at the place where she and Lucas had stood in their moment of near intimacy, and she realizes her mother had been watching the entire time. Abby's attention instantaneously shifts back to Karen.

"Were you spying on me?" Abby asks, clearly not pleased and already knowing the answer.

"No. I was cleaning, and then I happened to see you and Lucas out front—"

"Oh my God, you were! Why would you do that?"

"Abby, I am your mother, and it is my job to look after you…"

Karen pauses to gather her thoughts before proceeding, cautious not to push Abby too far, knowing she's already on the brink of erupting.

"I'm sorry, Abby. But after what happened with your father—"

"I'm not him."

"I know, Abby, but remember what the doctor said. I just don't want—"

"I know what he said, Karen."

"Then you know that's why we came out here."

"I said I know!"

Abby's mind races, and her nostrils flare. She tries to keep calm but loses control completely and screams at the top of her lungs. She then spins away and storms off down the hallway. In the process, she knocks a lamp off a nearby table, and the bulb shatters on the floor.

As Abby reaches her room, she places her hand on the doorknob but stops. She turns to look toward Karen. She scowls and glares menacingly at her mother. She shakes her head, letting her mother know she's made a mistake and that this may be her only warning. Satisfied Karen has understood her warning, Abby retreats into her bedroom.

Karen remains statuesque, unsure of what to do or how to handle her daughter and her outbursts without causing more.

CHAPTER 9

FALSE ALARM

Hovering over the black slate of a science-class table, Abby and Lucas gaze down at a skinned dead rat, spread apart as if being drawn and quartered and held in place by its feet pinned to a board. The classroom is filled with students, including Daniel and Jack, who are paired together in the rear of the classroom, ready to dissect their rat as well. Mr. Thompson, a teacher in his midforties, goes through the motions of instructing the kids on their assignment, knowing good and well most of them aren't paying attention.

"When you're finished, make sure your rat's organs are clearly marked with the pins I've provided, raise your hands, and I'll come by and take a look at what you have. And please—and I'm asking nicely—please keep all the parts of your rat in your rat, which means no flicking, no tossing, no grossing out your neighbor, and please no eating your rat."

The class giggles that Mr. Thompson needs to explain the obvious, though it's clearly necessary as Clifford, one of the boys in the class, fakes licking the rat to gross out the girl next to him.

"That means you," Mr. Thompson says to the boy, pointing him out to the rest of the class as an example of what not to do.

Lucas and Abby turn away from watching the boy's mischief and back to their own rat, ready to begin. Lucas lifts the scalpel from the table and hesitantly inches it closer to the rat but pulls away, unsure of where to begin.

"I thought you were a tough guy," Abby says, watching as Lucas wavers.

Ready to prove he's as tough as he acts, Lucas grips the scalpel, extends it toward the rat, gently presses the blade against it, and saws back and forth, barely making an incision. Abby looks on, her eyebrows raised, unimpressed by Lucas's weak attempt.

"Here," Abby says, growing impatient.

She takes the scalpel from Lucas's hand and places it on the table in front of her. Then she removes the ponytail holder from her wrist and places her hair up into a ponytail. With her hair now in place and out of the way, she takes the scalpel from the table and forces the rat down against the board to keep it from moving. She centers the blade between the rat's lower legs, slices it open to its chest, and places the scalpel back on table.

Without a second thought, she digs her thumbs into the incision and up under the ribs, snapping them one at a time, appearing to be enjoying herself as she does. Lucas looks on, his stomach turning, doing what he can to hide his nausea.

"There. Not so hard, is it?" Abby asks, still holding the ribs open.

"Yeah, I guess."

A retching sound from the rear of the class interrupts Abby and Lucas, also drawing the attention of the rest of the class. Mr. Thompson lowers the crossword puzzle from his face and kicks his feet down from his desk in time to see Jack barreling toward a trash can near the door and vomiting into it. As the class snickers at Jack and his inability to keep his lunch down, an exasperated Mr. Thompson is past the point of dealing with middle-school students and their consistent tomfoolery.

"Jack, please go to the nurse's office until you can find a way to control yourself."

With his head still buried in the trash can, Jack picks it up and exits the classroom, but not before dry heaving into the can once more, getting fewer chuckles than last time but more gasps of repulsion.

Daniel, who's now without a partner, turns his focus to Abby and Lucas, who, like the rest of the class, have their eyes on Jack as he leaves. Lucas glances back and spots Daniel glaring; he's obviously furious about the outcome of their last meeting at the baseball diamond the day before.

Choosing to avoid the conflict as usual, Lucas turns away from Daniel's glare and focuses on his rat. Abby, on the other hand, is less willing to fold, and she returns Daniel's glare, making a point of showing she has nothing to fear. Daniel, knowing he won't win this battle with her, gestures with an eye roll and a headshake. He decides that wasting his time with her isn't worth his effort.

Daniel goes back to his assignment, and Abby shifts her attention and gives Lucas a questioning look.

"You know if you keep letting him know you're afraid, he's gonna keep doing this, right?"

In true Lucas fashion, he keeps his head down, avoiding eye contact and doing what he can to avoid a confrontation.

"Whatever. Let's just finish this so we can be done."

"No. Not *whatever*. We should do something—"

Lucas reaches for the scalpel and lifts it from the table. Frustrated, Abby grabs it to rip it away but accidentally slices his hand. Wincing, Lucas instantly grips his hand. How could she, of all people, hurt him, even if by accident? Her terrified expression clearly shows this was far from intentional.

"I'm sorry. It was an accident; I promise," Abby says frantically.

"Whatever. Mr. Thompson, can I use the restroom?"

"If your rat is done, then yes. If it's not, then no," Mr. Thompson says.

"But, Mr. Thompson, I cut my hand, and it's bleeding."

"Take the hall pass." Mr. Thompson leaves his feet propped up on his desk and never lifts his head from his crossword puzzle.

"Lucas, I'm sorry," says Abby, feeling awful about hurting him.

Lucas, not wanting to hear any explanations, maneuvers past tables and chairs to the door, keeping pressure on his hand to prevent blood from dripping on the floor. He grabs an old Volkswagen emblem off the wall near the door on his way out.

Abby remorsefully watches Lucas as he exits with his hand bloodied, though not intentionally, by her forceful nature. Her head drops, but from the corner of her eye, she catches sight of Daniel in the rear of the class staring at her. She tilts her head toward him to get a better look. With a corrupt grin, Daniel puckers his lips and blows Abby a kiss. Infuriated, she responds by raising her middle finger to him. Daniel's grin is wiped away, and a look of disgust covers his face. He lifts his index finger and slides it across his throat with a vile glare, letting Abby know that the battle is about to begin.

"Mr. Thompson," he says. "I should probably bring Jack his things since it doesn't look like he's gonna be back." He grins as his eyes shift between Mr. Thompson and Abby.

"No lingering in the hallway, and after you bring him his things, bring yourself back," Mr. Thompson says, still preoccupied by his crossword puzzle.

Abby's suspicions grow to concerns as Daniel gathers all of Jack's personal belongings and shoves them into his backpack. He shoots Abby a wink on his way out the door.

⅄

Lucas is standing at the sink in the restroom and washing the blood from his hands when the sound of the door creaking open catches his attention. He looks in the mirror to see Daniel stroll through the door, wearing Jack's backpack and grinning from ear to ear. In a hurry, Lucas shuts the water off and grabs the hall pass, failing to dry his hands, hoping to flee before Daniel confronts him.

It's too late.

Daniel steps in front of him, preventing his escape.

"Where do you think you're going, Shit Stain?"

With his head down to avoid eye contact, Lucas makes another attempt to get to the door by stepping around Daniel. But Daniel sidesteps, blocking the exit once again. Standing directly in front of Daniel, Lucas finds himself face to face with his nemesis, who is staring him dead in the eyes.

"There's no bunnies in the boys' room, Burnout," Daniel says.

He uses an open palm to slam Lucas directly in the chest, sending him reeling across the bathroom and crashing against the wall. Grimacing in pain, Lucas scrambles to think of a way out, somewhere to run, but his only solution is in front of him—that is, through Daniel.

Lucas is cornered with nowhere to run, and Daniel is tired of being interrupted and having Lucas saved by circumstance; Daniel isn't going to squander this opportunity. He marches himself directly up to Lucas and thumps him in the stomach with a left uppercut, sending Lucas back against the wall and sliding to the floor.

Lucas struggles to regain his breath. Trying to gather himself, he manages to rise to a knee and watch as Daniel slips off Jack's backpack and unzips it, never averting his sinister stare. Daniel's stare becomes even more frightening as he reaches into Jack's backpack and retrieves what he was searching for.

Beep, beep, beep!

Startled by the blaring fire alarm, Daniel whips his head around to see a flashing light in the upper corner above the door. With Daniel briefly distracted, Lucas seizes the opportunity. He gets to his feet, kicks Daniel in the leg as hard as he can, and makes a mad dash for the door. Daniel, stunned for only a second, gives chase. Lucas reaches the bathroom door and flings it open. He runs about a foot before being bombarded by a crowd of students filing into the hallway. Hot on his heels, Daniel slams into Lucas's back but is unable to take care of his unfinished business because of the large number of witnesses now trolling the halls.

"Don't worry, Shit Stain. We're not done yet. And believe me, it's only gonna get worse," Daniel whispers into Lucas's ear while still pressed up against his back.

Lucas steps into the flow of traffic, leaving Daniel in the bathroom doorway, furious his plans have been foiled once again. Following the crowd down the hall, Lucas spots Mr. Thompson escorting Abby by the arm to the principal's office. Looking over her shoulder, searching through the crowd, Abby finds Lucas and gives him a wink followed by a smile.

Without a spoken word, Lucas knows she was there for him once more.

CHAPTER 10

THE LONG RIDE HOME

Planted in a chair outside the principal's office, Abby repeatedly snaps the ponytail holder around her wrist while she waits. Gripping it between two fingers, she slowly pulls it away from her wrist once more, testing the elasticity as it stretches to its breaking point. The principal's door opens, and Abby's head lifts to the door. The ponytail holder snaps back to her wrist, causing her to flinch.

Without uttering a word, Karen steps out of the principal's office and continues straight past Abby without acknowledging the existence of her only child. Knowing she's pushed her mother far past her limitations, Abby decides to wait a few seconds, giving her mother some space before following her out to the car.

Karen sits behind the steering wheel of her car, wiping tears from her eyes, struggling to deal with the product of her failed marriage and the continual misbehavior of her child. She's past the point of knowing what to do and begins to consider any other alternative than the ones that have failed her.

Abby knows she's in trouble. She slides into the passenger's side of the car, quietly shuts the door, and buckles herself in. She stares out the window and ponders a way to explain to her mother that this event was meant only to help Lucas avoid what was sure to be a brutal beating from Daniel.

"I'm sorry, Mommy," Abby says, turning to her mother. "I know what I did was wrong, but I did it for a good reason. There was this—"

"Save it, Abby." Karen is driving now and keeping her eyes on the road, no longer willing to entertain Abby's lackluster excuses.

"Where are we going?" Abby's not familiar with this particular part of town.

Her eyes looking dead ahead, Karen continues to drive, choking back tears. After another few minutes of silence, she slows the car, turns in to the parking lot of a small clinic, and parks. Abby, rising in her seat, realizes where she is and begins showing immediate signs of remorse for anything she's done, whether it be today or at any point in the past.

"I'm sorry, Mommy, please. Please don't make me go again," Abby says. "I promise I'll do better."

"I have to do something, Abby. I can't keep letting you do this. Look what happened to your father before we left," Karen says, tears falling from her face.

"I know, Mommy, but that's not what's happening this time; I swear. I really was trying to help Lucas. He was getting bullied again. I promise I'll change. I'll do whatever you want. Please don't make me stay at another one of these places again." Abby grabs her mother's hand, pleading for another chance.

"All that's great, Abby. But that doesn't explain how you've been treating me."

"I'm sorry, Mommy. Please give me another chance. It's been so hard without Dad. I'll prove I can change. And...and if I don't, you can bring me right back. I promise, cross my heart." Abby draws across her heart with her finger. "Let me show you."

Karen, feeling apprehensive about Abby's claim, looks up at her daughter, who's anxiously awaiting her decision. Thinking long and hard, reflecting on the events since the move, Karen makes her decision but doesn't yet speak the words to Abby, fearful it's the wrong decision.

To Abby's surprise, Karen puts her hand on the shifter and throws the car in reverse. Abby's grateful for her mother's willingness to give her not a second chance but another chance. She reaches across the seat and hugs her. With tears in her eyes, Karen returns her embrace, though not as tightly as a mother who was about to lose her only child for an unknown period should. Karen prays this decision doesn't haunt her or anyone else who may run across her daughter.

Lost in the moment, Karen neglects to remember she's put the car in reverse. As her foot lifts from the brake pedal, the car begins to roll back out of the parking space and toward an oncoming vehicle.

Honk! Honk!

Frightened by the blast of a car horn, Karen realizes her car is in motion. She slams on the brakes, bouncing Abby's head off the headrest. The car comes to an abrupt stop, narrowly missing a Volkswagen bus driven by a young hippie couple.

"The fuck?" The blond female passenger yells as she leans out the window, throwing her hands up out of frustration.

Karen apologetically waves and mouths the words *I'm sorry* to the young couple as they continue on, pissed off about their near collision, unaware that their lives are just days from being taken in the Alabama backwoods on a desolate road to nowhere.

Karen glances back at Abby, relieved she's avoided the accident yet still unconvinced she's made the correct decision. Before backing the rest of the way out of her parking spot, she sees the prominent sign of the local mental-health clinic, Shady Lane, in the rearview mirror, reminding her of the reasons she'd left California... To leave the past not only in the rearview mirror but in the past, where it belongs.

With a deep breath and a sigh, Karen backs out of her parking space, puts the car in drive, and pulls away. For the moment, Abby seems to have understood the severity of the situation and the consequences it could have.

CHAPTER 11

THE GIFT

Karen sits hunched over on her couch, lost in her thoughts, still reflecting on her decision to let Abby stay, unsure she's made the correct one. Thinking this move from California would be her escape from the past, she's discontent, realizing that even though she's made an attempt to run from her past, all she's done is bring it with her.

"'Bye, Mother," Abby says in her bubbly voice as she trots through the room to the front door.

"Sure, Abby, whatever you say," says Karen, staring into the distance, not paying attention to what Abby said—or that's she's even in the room, for that matter.

Abby, without a care in the world, swings the front door open, hops out, and closes the door behind her. Karen, lost in her own head, is taken from her thoughts by the slamming of the door. She glances toward it.

Gazing at the door, Karen stands from the couch, trudges into the kitchen, and opens the cabinet over the refrigerator. She reaches up, grabs a bottle of rum, and pulls it down. Giving the bottle a once-over, she stops for a moment, and her eyes shift back to the open cabinet filled with a few other bottles of liquor. She's in a trance; her eyes quiver as she stares, and her thoughts escape to other alternatives to her problem.

⚔

Popping out the front door with her high ponytail bobbing up and down, Abby skips a few steps toward Lucas, who's next door in his yard swinging his Louisville Slugger at a few small rocks, hitting them across the street. She slows from her skip as she approaches, curious about what exactly he's doing.

"Whatcha doin'?"

"Hittin' rocks." Lucas tosses another into the air and blasts it off the end of his bat, sending it bouncing down the street.

"Is it fun?"

Lucas shrugs and tosses another, letting it crack off the bat, sending it at least three houses down.

"Will you teach me?" Abby asks, thinking it's bizarre he doesn't use a ball.

Lucas stops what he's doing and rests the bat against his shoulder, focusing on Abby. He's worried someone might find out they were the ones responsible for the broken window out at Daniel's cabin.

"It's just throwing a rock up in the air and hitting it with a bat," he says. He glances around and anxiously leans in closer to Abby. "Ain't you worried someone might find out?"

"Nope," Abby says confidently. "We didn't do anything. Remember?"

Her eyes pierce deep into Lucas's. He takes a step back and stands tall, pretending to be as confident as she is.

"Me neither. I thought maybe you were," he says, not wanting her to see how fearful and insecure he really is.

"Sure," Abby says, not believing him for a second. "Anyway, I don't have time to be hittin' rocks right now on account I have to go get a present for my boyfriend." She watches Lucas's cheeks flush.

"What is it?"

"I'll give it to you later tonight. You can come out tonight, right?"

"Should be pretty easy. My mom has 'company' again tonight." Lucas does air quotes with his fingers.

"Cool."

"Not really."

"I mean that we can hang out."

"Oh. Yeah."

"Well, I'll see you later tonight then."

"'K."

Lucas stands in his yard, bat in hand, excited he'll be getting a gift from a girl for the first time. His mind wanders through the possibilities of what it might be as he watches Abby skip off down the street. Deciding not to think too much about it—as it's probably something girly anyhow—he lifts the bat from his shoulder, picks up another rock, tosses it into the air, and swings away.

Crack!

The rock flies off the end of the bat, whizzes through the air across the street, and barely misses a passing black car by just a few inches. The car's tires squeal against the asphalt as it comes to a screeching halt. Lucas freezes, making eye contact with the driver of the car, recognizing him as the stranger from the grocery store who returned his mother's dime.

The stranger observes Lucas closely. He lifts his foot off the brake and lets his car begin to roll forward and then past him, keeping his eyes on Lucas the entire time. Once the car rolls far enough for Lucas to be out of sight, Lucas drops his bat to the ground and backs up toward his house. He turns and runs in, worried about seeing the strange man multiple times in an otherwise small town where people aren't usually strangers for more than a day.

⅄

Near midnight, with a backpack strung over her shoulders, Abby stands outside Lucas's window, tapping on the glass. She looks around to make sure no one is out wandering. Receiving no answer, Abby grows impatient and taps on the window again, still peeking around the area.

"Come on," she says, mumbling to herself.

Fidgety, Abby starts bouncing up and down, hoping something hasn't happened to Lucas or, even worse, that he hasn't had a change of heart and lost interest in her.

There are no signs of life from the darkened room.

Abby, no longer able to contain herself and letting her anxiety get the best of her, cautiously inspects the area once more and takes a step closer. She takes a deep breath, cups her hands around her face, and places them against the window. She's fearful of what might lie behind the glass and closed blinds.

Zip!

Lucas's blinds fly open. Abby stumbles backward, trips over herself, and falls onto her rear. Lucas slides his window open and climbs out as Abby picks herself up and dusts off her clothes, still recovering from her scare.

"Ready," says Lucas with a smirk, knowing he's scared Abby half to death but deciding he'll let it be. After all, she's got a gift waiting for him.

"Yeah, but I think I'm gonna finish dying of a heart attack real quick first," she says, clutching her chest. Lucas's smirk grows.

"What's in the backpack? Is it my present?"

"I guess you'll have to wait and see."

Abby gives Lucas a hint of a smile, which he echoes. She grabs him by the hand and leads him toward the woods behind their homes, knowing her present to him is one he'll never forget.

⟁

Abby continues to lead Lucas deep into the woods down a trail, dodging tree limbs and brush and heading in a direction he's less than unfamiliar with. Realizing that Abby's veered from the path that takes them to the old mill-pond, Lucas fears becoming lost.

"This isn't the way," he says, searching the area for any familiar landmarks.

"Yes, it is." Abby's confident.

"No, it's not. The pond is over that way." Lucas points in the opposite direction.

"Yes, it is. We're not going to the pond."

"OK. Then where are we going?"

"I told you. I got you something. Remember?" Abby feels a tad less confident after Lucas's persistence.

In a moment of uncertainty, she takes a good look at her surroundings, making sure she is in fact heading in the right direction. She then spots a familiar sight, clueing her in that she's chosen the right path, and forges on.

Hearing about his gift once again, Lucas follows her. He doesn't care where they go, as long as his gift is at the end of that rainbow.

"Is it in the backpack?" He pushes a few branches to the side and squeezes past, still trailing Abby.

"You'll see when we get there." Ironically, *she's* becoming irritated by *his* constant questions.

"Well, how far is it?"

"I thought you didn't like a lot of questions."

Lucas is caught off guard and shrugs. "Probably learned it from you."

"We should be pretty close now," Abby says, keeping her focus forward.

Lucas snatches Abby by the arm, and they freeze. All his senses become amplified as he goes on high alert, his eyes rapidly scanning the area.

"What?" asks Abby.

Lucas shushes her.

"I thought I heard something," he whispers.

Abby and Lucas take some time to listen for any foreign sounds but hear nothing out of the ordinary, only the sounds of the forest. Abby shakes her head at Lucas and continues to march on. But she takes only a few steps before he races after her and stops her once more, holding up a finger, advising Abby to stay silent.

A muffled voice not too far off in the distance sends Lucas into a panic. He rapidly searches through the darkness, fearful they're no longer alone.

"I told you. Now let's go," Lucas says in a shaky voice, ready to tuck tail and run.

Abby fearlessly takes a step closer to Lucas, watching as he freaks out and gets ready to scramble at the sight of whoever may be lurking nearby.

"Are you scared?" she confidently asks.

Lucas compses himself, backtracking on his answer in an attempt to show her he's not actually afraid but more concerned about her welfare.

"No. I was thinking of you. I don't want you having nightmares or whatever."

Abby takes another step toward him, clutches a handful of his shirt, and drags him in the direction she's been leading him. Though Lucas is attempting to show more confidence, or as much as one can show while being dragged around by a twelve-year-old girl, he's still visibly tense as they begin to close in on the mumbling. Lucas soon recognizes it as crying.

⅄

Abby drags Lucas around a large bush and into a small clearing. Her flashlight illuminates the area until it focuses on a single location.

A teenage boy or young man is seated with his back against the base of a tree. His arms are tied around it, and a black burlap sack covers his head, muffling the breathing. With his attention focused on the captive, Lucas missteps and falls to the ground. But his eyes never waver. He springs back to his feet and dusts himself off, just as quickly as he fell.

"Abby, what's going on?"

The captive's muffled cries intensify.

"It's your present," Abby says, cheerfully smirking.

Abby takes a few steps to the tree and rips the burlap sack from the person's head. It's Daniel. Tears run down his face, and he blubbers beneath the peeling duct tape covering his mouth.

"Shut up!" Abby says into Daniel's face, her voice going from sweet to vicious in a heartbeat. Unfortunately for Daniel, he continues to snivel uncontrollably, provoking Abby to kick dirt into his face. "I said shut up!"

"Why is he like this, Abby?" Lucas asks, confused.

Abby towers over him, scowling.

"Because he's stupid. A dumb, stupid boy who thinks it's OK to pick on people who can't do anything to defend themselves," Abby furiously states in blubbering Daniel's face.

"What…what are you going to do to him?"

Abby unslings the backpack from over her shoulders and flings it back at Lucas, striking him in the chest.

"Open it," she says, keeping her sinister glare on Daniel.

Lucas fumbles to open the backpack, dividing his attention between it and Daniel. With trembling hands, he manages to unzip the bag and peek inside. He finds a Polaroid camera, a knife, loose makeup, markers, and a bag of crackers.

"I don't get it."

Abby lets out an exhausted sigh as she contorts her body to look at Lucas. Seeing his fear and confusion, she turns all her attention back to him and reverts to being the sweet girl next door. She walks over to him, takes the backpack, and starts removing the items one at a time, explaining the intention behind each.

"Here, I'll show you, silly. The makeup is so we can make him look like the little girl he is." She raises her voice with each word as she looks back over her shoulder at Daniel, letting him know she's the one who should be feared. Looking at Lucas again, Abby sweetens her voice. "The camera is so we can get a picture of our pretty girl."

Abby drops the camera into the backpack and pauses. She smiles as her eyes fixate on the knife at the bottom. She reaches in and pulls it from the backpack by the handle, twirling it back and forth, mesmerized by the flashlight's shimmering reflection on the blade.

"And this...this is to cut him loose when we're done," she says, now smiling as if this were just any other day.

"What about the crackers?" Lucas asks, still perplexed about how he got himself into this situation.

"Hello? In case we get hungry. I really shouldn't have to explain that one." Abby rolls her eyes and drops the knife into the backpack.

"This isn't right, Abby," Lucas says.

Sweet Abby turns sour and slightly aggressive, but only to get her point across that if Lucas doesn't stand up for himself, he may as well remain seated forever.

"What's not right—the way he pushed you around? The name-calling? Or just the bullying in general?" Abby repositions herself over Daniel, letting her villainous tone express her disgust with Daniel and his recent behavior. "We're gonna get a picture. That way, if he's ever mean again, we can show the whole school he's nothing but a crybaby sissy girl." She inches closer to

Daniel's face with every word. "And that's why we're gonna be nice! Right, little girl?" Daniel eagerly nods. "Now let's do this girl's makeup."

Abby, staring deep into Daniel's eyes, reaches her hand behind her back with her palm up, waiting for Lucas to place some of the makeup into it. Still waiting, she wiggles her fingers, signaling to Lucas that he's taking too long. Nothing. Puzzled, she rises and turns back to find him so lost in thought that he hasn't realized she was trying to get his attention.

"Ugh, forget it. I'll do it myself," she says, knowing Lucas isn't going to be much help.

She snatches the backpack from him and pulls it open. Reaching in, she extracts the knife. She admires every inch of it as she gradually spins back toward Daniel, her eyes leaving the knife to meet his.

"I think I may have a better idea," she says.

Daniel, seeing the knife and the twisted look in Abby's eyes, shakes his head in fear.

Abby raises the knife and flings it forward.

"Abby, no!" says Lucas.

The knife strikes the ground blade first, leaving the handle up, just as Abby wanted it.

"No what?" she asks.

"Nothing."

"Okay. Now can you please come hold the bag for me?"

Lucas loosens up a bit and steps to Abby's side. He takes the backpack, realizing they're not out here for any reason other than the opportunity to embarrass Daniel and free Lucas from the daily fear of being bullied. Abby nonchalantly removes the ponytail tie from around her wrist, throws her hair up into a ponytail, and starts grabbing markers from the bag one at a time. She begins her masterpiece on Daniel by starting with a nose and then moving on to the whiskers. But Daniel struggles, turning his head to prevent her from drawing. After a few failed attempts, Abby's fed up. She grabs a handful of his hair and rips his head straight back to her.

"Stop moving!"

A sniveling Daniel decides it's best to comply and get it over with, letting Abby finish her drawing. Completely satisfied, Abby steps away from him and admires her work, letting her vicious grin shine.

"Who's the bunny now?" she asks Daniel, smirking.

Lucas, who only a short time ago was full of fear, has found himself enjoying this reversal of roles. His fears have completely receded, and he breaks into laughter at the bunny before him.

"I'm glad you like your present," says Abby.

"It's the best," he says, giggling at Daniel.

Abby takes the camera out of the backpack, aligns herself with Daniel, and begins taking a few pictures. After looking at a few of the results and not being pleased by any of them, she crouches down near Daniel's face to get a close-up.

But Lucas stops her.

"Wait! Take off the tape so we can get a good one," he says.

Abby agrees, reaches over to Daniel, and rips the tape off his mouth.

"Please just let me go," he says through his tears.

Abby sneers. "If you ever wanna leave this tree, you're gonna shut your bunny mouth."

"Yeah, Bunny," says Lucas, chiming in with his two cents. He feels braver with Daniel tied to a tree and his face painted like a bunny.

Abby and Lucas step back from Daniel and take a few more pictures until they're pleased they have enough leverage against him. Abby drops the camera back into the backpack and approaches Daniel, whose tears have now caused the marker ink to begin streaking down his face.

"Now when I let you go, you're gonna be nice, right," says Abby, more stating this fact rather than asking.

"Yes, yes, I swear. Please let me go home. I swear I'll be nice," says Daniel. He's ready to do anything he's asked at this point to get set free.

"And remember that if you don't, everyone's gonna see your pretty bunny face. Are we clear?"

Nodding, with tears running down his face, Daniel attempts to compose himself the best he can. Abby reaches down, grips the knife, and plucks it from the ground. She closes in on Daniel and takes a knee in front of him, crowding his face and lifting the knife within inches of his cheek.

"And you're not gonna tell anyone either, are you?"

"I promise. I'll never tell anyone."

"Good. And it better stay that way, or else." Abby waits to see whether Daniel responds. "What's the matter? You don't wanna know or else what?"

She smirks as Daniel rapidly shakes his head, making sure he doesn't give her a reason to keep him tied to the tree any longer. Convinced Daniel's days of bullying are over, Abby reaches the knife behind the tree to cut him loose. Daniel breathes a huge sigh of relief as he slowly calms, knowing his nightmare is just about over.

Strands of rope snap and pull apart as Abby saws away with the knife. Suddenly she stops. Her eyes drift into the dark forest as if she's seen a ghost, and she gives a slow nod. Her eyes veer back to Daniel, and with a desolate glare, she places the blade to his throat and slides it across. His neck splits open and spills blood down the front of his shirt.

Daniel's eyes widen as he unsuccessfully gasps for air. His eyes gradually flutter and begin to close as his body weakens. His head bobs and finally falls, going limp and slumping over, while his body is still tied to the tree.

Lucas trembles, shocked at the horror he's just witnessed.

"Why?" He's barely able to speak.

"It had to be done, Lucas. Now help me cut him loose."

"Abby, no. What did you do? I can't—" He stops talking when Abby charges toward him with the bloodied knife.

Retreating as quickly as he can, away from Abby's onslaught, Lucas runs smack into a tree. Abby positions herself face to face with him, while blood drips from the blade at her side.

"We're in this together, whether you like it or not! Your dad's not coming back, your mom hates you, and I'm your only friend."

His head buzzing with pain and horror, Lucas is now faced with the killer herself, who up until this point was the only friend he's had. Stunned and hurt by Abby's outburst, he has to decide what to do next, and he has to do it now.

Abby, realizing Lucas is rethinking every second he's spent with her and is currently contemplating his next move, catches him giving a quick glance at the knife. Prepared to do whatever it takes to save her skin, she takes a step and reassesses her approach.

"I'm sorry. That came out wrong. I meant that all we have is each other." She drops the knife onto the ground, showing she would never intentionally harm him. With her head down and her shoulders slumped, she takes a step toward Lucas, who flinches as she raises her hand to his neck. But he then settles down, realizing she's just reaching for the pendant around his neck and lifting it for him to see.

"In it together. Remember? That's what you said."

Abby lets the pendant fall back onto Lucas's chest and reaches out to take his hand. She stares into his eyes and waits for a response.

Lucas searches searchingly into Abby's eyes. Was her apology genuine or an insidious way of manipulating him into doing her dirty work? On top of the gruesomely disgusting behavior and her spiteful words thrown in his face, he still has one more problem.

Abby's right.

Lucas starts to control his breathing and then closes his eyes in a prolonged, dreary blink.

"In it together," he says.

"Really?" Abby's eyes fill with excitement and glee.

Lucas gives a tentative nod.

"Yay!" Abby jumps up and down and claps. "Now let's cut him loose, and we'll drag him down to the pond and throw him in."

Lucas, still unable to step forward, watches Abby celebrate his willingness to be an accomplice to murder. In the darkness that is no longer just the forests night he now knows he's willing to do anything and everything to keep the only friend he's ever had.

Abby walks over to Daniel's lifeless body, reaches around the tree, and finishes cutting him free of his restraints. He buckles in half and flops to the ground. After cutting the body loose, Abby gathers her things and places them into the backpack. Lucas stares at Daniel's crumpled corpse and offers no assistance, but Abby seems perfectly fine cleaning up her own mess.

Staring curiously into the backpack, Abby reaches in and is pleased to find her package of crackers. Without a care in the world and completely disregarding the situation she's created, she opens the package and tosses a cracker into her mouth. With her mouth full, she glances up at Lucas, catching him wide eyed and staring at her ability to eat, considering the circumstances.

"I told you the crackers were a good idea," Abby says. "Now grab an arm."

Abby tosses the crackers into the backpack and approaches Daniel's body. She grabs an arm and pulls him from the tree, but fails to move him very far. Lucas continues to keep his distance while watching Abby work.

Knowing she'll need Lucas's help, Abby lets the body flop to the ground and turns her attention back to Lucas.

"If I give you a cracker, will you help?" She knows that won't be the deciding factor. "Will you please come help me?"

Reengaging himself, Lucas awkwardly joins her. Each of them grabs an arm and starts tugging away. Exhausted and struggling to pull the weight of the body, they make it only about forty feet before dropping back to the ground. Daniel's heels have dug into the earth, leaving ruts and blood-stained topsoil behind.

Abby's panting. "We're never gonna make it there. Besides, they're just gonna follow this trail right to the pond anyway."

"We can't leave him here," Lucas says, worried the body will be found by morning.

"Sure we can."

"But, Abby, we have to do something."

"We are. We're going home."

"I meant with the body."

"No, we don't."

Out of frustration and pure hysteria, Lucas grabs Daniel by the wrists and pulls as hard as he can, his feet digging into the dirt. But he loses his grip and slips as he strains, barely moving the body a few inches.

"Stop," Abby says, placing a hand on Lucas's shoulder.

"But they'll find him, and then they'll find us," Lucas says, giving one last jerk.

"So? Let them find the body."

Lucas lets go. He stands over the body, disoriented, confused, and scared. He runs his fingers through his hair, unsure how to comprehend the severity of the situation. Abby has zero problems with the significance of the evening's events but is receptive to the idea that this is Lucas's first murder She figures his conscience is surely telling him what he did is wrong, but what he needs is his friend at his side showing him everything will be OK.

"Look. If we leave him here, yes, someone will find him. But no one will ever know it was us. They'll probably think it was some local child molester, pedo, feeler, whatever guy, and we'll be fine. Trust me."

While Lucas is fixated on the body, Abby gathers the backpack and takes his hand in hers. Breaking his stare, Lucas turns to Abby, who steps over Daniel's body as they flee the scene. As they step into the woods, Lucas takes one last glance back into the clearing at the gruesome scene that can never be undone.

Abby never looks back.

CHAPTER 12

Ice-Cold Lemonade

Slouched on the couch in his living room with his feet up on a cluttered coffee table, eating a generic brand of cereal from a Tupperware bowl, Lucas is absorbed in the world of Saturday-morning cartoons. The old tube television reflects a blue hue across the room. As much as he'd like to ignore the muffled voices, they continue to echo from his mother's room down the hall and drown out the cartoons. He glances in that direction, frustrated he's no longer able to concentrate on his once-a-week show, *The Flintstones*.

Taking another bite of his cereal, Lucas pushes a few things around the coffee table to make room for his bowl and sets it down. He pulls himself up from the couch, trudges over to the living-room window, and pries the blinds open. He sees something unexpected.

A sheriff's patrol car is parked out front.

Panic begins setting in as Lucas backs away from his window. He looks back toward his mother's door and hears the muffled voices behind the walls. He plants himself on the edge of the couch, wondering how they could have found out so quickly.

Click.

Donna's bedroom door opens. Lucas's heart races, pounding from his chest and into his temples. Donna enters the hallway wearing only a white bathrobe, and her hair is a complete mess. Deputy Morgan follows behind her, gear belt in hand and his shirt only half-buttoned. Lucas finally exhales, not realizing he had been holding his breath. For the first time in his life, he's pleased to see the man in his house was there only because of his mother's promiscuity. Lucas's fears alleviated, he grabs his bowl from the coffee table and sinks himself back into the couch and the glow of his Saturday-morning cartoons.

"Ain't you gonna say hi?" Donna asks Lucas as she and the deputy enter the living room. Lucas slows his chewing, and his eyes shift from his mother to Deputy Morgan. "Damn it, Lucas Dean Wright! You better speak!"

"Hi," Lucas says through a mouthful of cereal.

Donna shuffles a few things around on the cluttered coffee table until she finds her cigarettes. She removes the pack from the table and opens it, taking one out and placing it between her lips.

Deputy Morgan clears his throat. "Now you listen here, boy. I'm gonna let it slide this time. But before you know it, I might be your new daddy, and things are bound to change. You copy that?"

Lucas stops chewing and gives a solid nod.

"You're damn right they're gonna change," Donna mumbles as she lights the cigarette dangling from her mouth.

Deputy Morgan starts for the door with Donna behind him, but he pauses for a moment as a thought pops into his mind. He turns back to Lucas.

"You don't by chance know anything about a broken window out by the old Stetson place, do you, boy?"

"No," says Lucas, his eyes about to burst from his head as he swallows hard.

"No what?" Donna asks.

"No, sir," he says, adrenaline once again taking over.

Glaring at Lucas, Donna lets her attention slip back to the deputy and pulls him in close. Lucas looks on uncomfortably as they press their bodies together, speak in unintelligible voices, and kiss each other between words. Donna gives a little jump when the frisky deputy pinches her rear. Sensing Lucas's stare, Donna rolls her eyes at him, and he instantly turns back to the television, not wanting to witness his mother's behavior. Yet as with a horrific car accident, it's hard to turn away.

Deputy Morgan kisses Donna one last time, and they say their good-byes. He then heads out the door and moves on with his day.

After Deputy Morgan makes his way out, Donna closes the door behind him. She storms over to Lucas and snatches him up off the couch by his arm.

"I'm sick and tired of you acting like such a little shit all the time. You're going to your room, and you're stayin' in there the rest of the day!"

Donna, fuming, with her fingers wrapped tightly enough around Lucas's arm to leave a bruise, jerks him across the coffee table, bumping it and spilling the milk from his bowl of cereal. "Now look what you gone and done. I have the right mind to send you to live with your father."

Having heard this line from her at every moment she's found the opportunity to throw it in his face, Lucas has finally heard it one too often. He yanks his arm away and lashes out.

"Do it then!" he screams into her face.

With a half-lit cigarette pressed between her lips, Donna strikes Lucas across the cheek with an open palm. Lucas is left standing in awe, and he watches as his mother's fury builds. She plucks the cigarette from her mouth and stamps it out in an ashtray on the coffee table.

"If this is the kinda shit you wanna pull, you ain't even gettin' your room," she says.

Donna drags him out of the living room and down the hall, where she gives him a shove, sending him stumbling backward into the bathroom. Regaining his balance, Lucas stares back at his mother, broken and confused. What has he done wrong?

"This is your room now!" Donna says.

The bathroom door slams in Lucas's face. His eyes swell and tear, his teeth clench, and his knuckles turn white as his fists tighten. Rage builds and courses through his veins; he's ready to explode.

"I hate you!" he screams at the top of his lungs while banging on the door. "I…HATE…YOU!"

Lucas's screams turn to sobs as he breaks; his shoulders slump forward, and tears fall from his face. Turning from the door, he finds his discontented and infuriated reflection in the mirror. He wipes at his tears as he stares into his own bloodshot, swollen eyes. He's able to see the rage and resentment he feels for his mother visibly flaring, ready to escape.

"You're just like your father, Lucas," he says to himself, mimicking Donna. "Go live with your father, Lucas. You're a piece of shit, Lucas. You're a piece of shit! I fucking hate you!"

Lucas glares at himself, disgusted by what he sees.

"What are you looking at? Yeah, you. Maybe if you weren't such a pussy, neither of us would have to deal with her shit, you fucking pussy!"

Lucas's lip begins to quiver as the tears once again fall from this broken, lonely boy. He has no father, no real mother, and only recently found his first true friend. He turns away from the mirror, no longer able to stomach his own reflection; places his back against the door; and lets himself slide to the floor, hiding his face between his arms, which are crossed over his knees. He weeps.

⋏

Abby springs from her front door with her jump rope in hand, but she comes to an abrupt stop at the sight of the deputy's car parked in front of Lucas's house. Lucas's front door opens, stealing her attention as Deputy Morgan steps out and strolls to his car like a man who knows he's in control. His head rotates toward Abby, who's as still as a deer in headlights, letting only her eyes follow him. What's he doing at Lucas's house?

The deputy slides himself into the driver's side of the car and takes another look back at Abby, sizing her up, curious about one of the new faces in town. Abby watches as he raises his mic to his lips and speaks into it, all the while analyzing Abby. She hears unintelligible radio chatter through the patrol car's window. Deputy Morgan then gives Abby a slow nod and drives off down the street.

Monitoring the situation closely, Abby waits until the car is far enough down the street, and then she does an instant 180-degree turn. She drops her rope and makes a beeline for Lucas's door. She wants to find out what exactly is going on, and she wants to find out now.

Abby stands on Lucas's front step, her arms crossed and foot tapping, impatiently waiting for Lucas to answer. She quickly becomes all smiles when it's Donna who answers the door rather than Lucas.

"Hi, Ms. Wright. Can Lucas come out and play?"

"I'm sorry, darling, but Lucas can't play today. He's gone and got himself into some trouble."

"Oh. OK. Thanks anyway," Abby says, letting her smile fade.

Donna closes the door. Abby rounds the corner of Lucas's house, wanting to know verbatim what Lucas has told the deputy to get himself in trouble. She makes her way straight to his bedroom window and gives it a few taps, prepared to lay into him for whatever it is he said or did that attracted the deputy to his house in the first place.

Her blood is already boiling, and her patience is growing thinner as she waits, thinking of all the information Lucas may have already volunteered to the deputy. About to rap on his window once more, she's interrupted by the sound of crying from the next window over. She timidly approaches, slightly calming down, and becomes more concerned that Lucas may need help.

Abby gives the window a few soft taps, hoping that it is Lucas's cries she hears. As the window creaks open, she takes a vigilant step back, unsure of what to expect. Lucas leans out, his face red and filled with the after effects of his crying fit. Abby relaxes, but only for a split second.

"What's going on, and why was there a cop at your house, Lucas?" Abby asks, not beating around the bush.

"He spent the night with my mom," Lucas says, still sniffling.

"So, are you, like, hiding or something?" Abby feels relieved that the deputy hadn't been there for them.

"No. She's making me stay in here. We can do something tomorrow."

"Who? Your mom?"

"Yeah, my mom; who else? She got mad when I—"

"You better pipe down in there," Donna yells from another room.

"I'll take care of it," Abby says, storming off, no longer needing to hear the rest.

"What are you gonna do? Abby? Psst. Abby?"

Lucas's attempts to get Abby's attention fruitless as she rounds the corner and moves out of view, leaving him hanging out of the bathroom window, wondering exactly what her intentions are this time—especially after last night.

⋏

Abby rummages through her kitchen, searching one cabinet after another, unable to find what she's looking for. She turns to the drawers and starts pulling them open one at a time, shuffling through each until she spies something in the far corner of the counter and behind one of the boxes. She smiles as she methodically reaches behind the box and removes an enormous kitchen knife. She becomes lost in her own reflection in the blade.

"I was looking for you," she says, titling the knife back and forth, examining every inch of it, running her fingers up and down the blade, and humming a familiar tune. Still stroking the blade, she spins around and marches across the room. Standing over her victim, she raises the knife and, with immense force, slashes downward.

The knife makes contact, splitting her victim in two.

Abby happily grabs half of the lemon on the cutting board, places it on a lemon juicer above a glass pitcher, and squeezes, watching the juice drip into the pitcher below. She tosses the spent side of the lemon aside and dips down eye level with the pitcher.

"Don't worry. Your friends will be joining you soon," she says in an eerie voice.

⋏

Abby carefully carries a tray holding a pitcher of lemonade and two filled glasses across her lawn toward Lucas's front door just as Karen pulls up in front of her house. She takes a second to watch Abby through her windshield, wondering what exactly her daughter is doing, until Abby glances back at her with an all-too-familiar grin. Panic sets in. Karen bolts from her car and scurries to Abby in an attempt to reach her and put a stop to whatever it is her twisted mind has her up to this time.

"What's going on, Abby?" Karen asks, hurrying toward her.

"Nothing, Mother. Just bringing some lemonade to Ms. Wright." Abby's annoyed her mother's already trying to interfere.

Reaching Lucas's front porch before her mother can reach her, Abby knocks on the front door.

"Is there a reason?" Karen asks, stepping up to the porch behind her.

"Just being a good neighbor," Abby says, putting on a fake smile as Donna opens the door.

"I'm sorry, Abby, but Lucas still can't play," Donna says before noticing Karen behind her. "Oh, hey. How you doin'?"

"I know Lucas is in trouble, but you looked upset earlier, so I thought I'd make you some lemonade," Abby says, with the sweet smile of the good girl next door.

"How sweet," Donna says.

With a developing smirk, Abby lowers her eyes to one particular condensation-covered glass of lemonade on the tray. As Karen observes Abby, anticipating her next move, she swoops in and snags that glass before Abby reaches it. Abby's smirk transforms into a spite-filled scowl as her head whips toward Karen. She knows her mother is purposefully trying to sabotage her plan.

"I'll have a glass," Karen says.

"That one was for Ms. Wright, Mother," Abby says maliciously while attempting to keep her faux smile shining.

"It's fine, sweetie," Donna says. "I'll just take this one." She grabs the other glass and takes a sip. "Oh my word, this is fabulous. Thank you, sweetheart. Karen, have you tried this yet? It is something else."

Abby's shark smile widens. "Yeah. Try it, Mother."

Feeling uneasy, Karen glances between Donna and Abby, who both eagerly wait her opinion on Abby's top-notch beverage. Suspicious, Karen lifts the glass to her lips and tilts it back far enough to give the appearance she's tasting it without ever letting the liquid come into contact with her lips. She then lowers it and fake swallows.

"That really is good," Karen says, fooling Donna but not Abby.

"I wish Lucas was that well behaved," Donna says, looking for confirmation of how great Abby is. Karen responds only with the flicker of a smile, scoffing at the idea that Donna is under the impression Abby is the ideal child.

"I'm glad you like it. Let me top your glass off," Abby says.

"You ain't gotta do all that," Donna says.

"Let's not be bothering her now, Abby," Karen says.

"I'll bring you some more tomorrow then," Abby says and parades back to her house, balancing the pitcher on the tray.

Karen sighs. "Sorry about that. You can bring the glass back whenever." She's worried about what else Abby's up to.

"It's OK, hun. She's just tryin' to be friendly."

"Sure," Karen says in a daze, keeping an eye on Abby until she's back inside her house. "OK, well, I guess I better get back."

"Of course. 'Bye, hun."

Donna waves to Karen and closes the door. Karen hurries back to her house, pouring the lemonade out on the lawn on her way, confident Abby's done something to it—but what exactly, she's unsure.

⅄

Abby stands in her kitchen pouring the pitcher of lemonade down the drain, seething at her mother's meddling. Karen bursts through the door, holding her empty glass and ready to confront her. Abby stops what she's doing and glowers at her.

"Don't do this to me again, Abby. You need to tell me what's going on," Karen says on the brink of tears.

"All I was trying to do was be nice, but like you never trusted Dad, you don't trust me," Abby says, barking crudely.

She pushes her way past Karen and begins to exit the kitchen but stops just before she does. She turns her head and looks back over her shoulder.

"Were you thirsty, Mother?"

Abby lets her comment soak into her mother's subconscious as she walks away. Karen wonders where she went wrong and why she didn't leave Abby at the clinic. Abby would be safe there, as well as anyone else who comes in contact with her. Beside herself, Karen tilts her glass, which is empty except

89

for a grainy substance lining its bottom She notices a container of sugar left out on the counter, near the lemon juicer, and realizes it may be her own paranoia that's driving her daughter to retaliate the way she does. Feeling guilty, she places her glass in the sink and bumps her knee on the cabinet under it, for it's not completely closed. In fact it's held open by a box of rat poison that wasn't pushed back far enough.

Karen's paranoia may have been plausible.

CHAPTER 13

THE CONFESSION

Sitting on her front porch, her eyes fixated on the deputy's car parked in front of Lucas's house, Abby bounces a red rubber ball, repetitively catching it as she considers the many boulevards by which she can remove him from the equation. Lucas's front door swings open, drawing her attention. She snatches the ball from the air and watches as Deputy Morgan escorts Lucas from his house and to the patrol car.

Suspicious, Abby stares as they reach the car. Deputy Morgan opens the passenger's side door for Lucas and places him inside. While the deputy walks around to the driver's side, Abby catches Lucas peeking back at her. He grins and winks, letting her know he's got it all under control.

Abby, more confused than before, is at least satisfied that she has nothing to worry about. Now on the driver's side, the deputy opens his door but pauses before climbing in. He rests his forearms on the roof of his car as he looks at Abby. To defuse the situation and put any concerns the deputy might have about her at ease, Abby dons a fake second-grade smile, overly excited, and waves, showing the deputy she's nothing but the sweet, innocent girl next door who'd never do anything worse than interrupt his Sunday football game in an attempt to sell him cookies.

Satisfied with his assessment, Deputy Morgan smiles, tips his hat, slips into the car, and closes the door behind him. As the deputy drives away, Lucas keeps his eyes on Abby until he can no longer see her.

Abby knows Lucas well enough at this point to know he's up to something, but she's unsure of what yet. She plays a few scenarios in her head and smiles. She then gives her ball one last hard bounce and snatches it from the air as she jumps to her feet and runs back into her house, letting the screen door slam behind her.

◢

In no particular hurry, Deputy Morgan drives through the backwoods and down the old dirt path leading to Daniel's cabin. Lucas stares out his window at the passing trees, trying to avoid conversation while he continuously visualizes the next few moments in his head, making sure they play out according to plan.

"You're lucky your mom and I are an item," the deputy says. "Let's just say if it wasn't for me, you'd be lookin' at a whole new scenario 'bout now."

"I know," Lucas says, his eyes still fixed out the window.

Spotting Daniel's cabin coming into view, Lucas takes a deep breath and prepares himself as the deputy turns into the driveway and puts the car in park.

Lucas begins his apology.

"I'm sorry, sir. I know it was stupid an' all; then once I did it, well, I started to feel bad, and that's why I told you."

"I'm glad you did. That right there's the first step of becoming a man— learning to admit when you've made a mistake. It doesn't change the fact you're still gonna have to pay for that window, but it's a good first step." Deputy Morgan does his best to prove his parenting abilities.

"Yes, sir. I sure am glad my mom likes you. It's been really hard for us since my dad left, and it'd be nice to have...I don't know...someone like, just, like around. You know?"

"Well, that's very kind of you to say. Now, let's get this apology done, and put all this behind us."

As they exit the car, Lucas lets his fake smile shine, as he couldn't be more pleased with his performance. Deputy Morgan approaches the front door of the cabin but halts, noticing Lucas isn't at his side but has begun to wander off toward the woods.

"Where are you going?" the deputy asks, becoming skeptical of Lucas's now nervous behavior.

"I was just gonna show you where I threw the rock from," Lucas says, becoming flustered, knowing there's the possibility the deputy may find out about Daniel's death.

"Why don't we talk to Mr. Stetson first, and then we'll take a look around."

"Yes, sir," Lucas says, nervously following him to the door.

As they approach the front door, the deputy leans to the side, taking a good look at the broken window before he knocks. After a good solid knock on the door, Lucas and the deputy wait, getting no answer. The deputy glances around the property and notices Mr. Stetson's truck. Knowing he's home, he knocks again. Glancing down, he does a double take at the ground beneath his feet and bends to take a closer look. He runs his fingers across what looks like bloodstains and skid marks from something having been dragged into the cabin.

As he reaches for his walkie-talkie, he sees Lucas standing tall and facing the door, his eyes closed, his body tensed and braced, and his teeth clenched.

Crack!

A Louisville Slugger shatters the back of the deputy's skull, splattering the door with blood. Lucas reluctantly opens his eyes and gazes at the deputy as he lies on the ground squirming and gasping for air, his head covered in blood, fighting to stay alive.

⁂

Exhausted and covered in blood splatters, Lucas jogs from the tree line behind his house to the space between his and Abby's homes. He unwinds the garden hose, cranks on the water, runs it over his head, and sprays off his clothes to remove as much blood as possible. Deciding he'll never completely remove the blood from his shirt, he peels it off, tosses it to the ground, and runs the hose back over his head and chest, washing away as much blood as he can.

Abby hears the ruckus from her bedroom window and pulls her curtain back just enough to get a glimpse of Lucas scrambling shirtless to wash himself as discreetly as possible. Aroused, Abby is nothing less than delighted to see her boyfriend taking matters into his own hands and eliminating a potential problem in her master plan to be with him at all costs.

Thinking he's heard a noise, Lucas springs into an upright position, scanning the area for witnesses to make sure he hasn't been seen. Satisfied the coast is clear, he shuts off the hose, leaves it strewn about, balls up his bloodied shirt, and shoves it into a small crack under his house, giving it a few kicks to ensure it's completely out of view before running off toward the front of his house. Abby follows him with her eyes as far as she can before letting her curtains close. She stands tall and proud of her new boyfriend and his fortitude.

⚓

Bursting through his front door, soaking wet and shirtless, Lucas slams into Donna, who's standing in the living room with her hands out to her sides. She shakes off the water Lucas so inconsiderately shared.

"What in the hell are you doin'?" Donna asks, about to lay into Lucas again.

"I'm sorry, ma'am. I fell in a big mud puddle on my way back. I tried to wash it off outside before I came in so I wouldn't make a mess in the house."

"And what do you call this? And why didn't Deputy Morgan drop you off?" Donna throws her hands up onto her hips, awaiting another poor excuse from Lucas.

Not having thought about running into his mother this way, Lucas hadn't prepared himself or a story for this unanticipated run-in.

"He...um...he said he had to do some police stuff, so I had to walk. I'll go grab a towel right now."

"Damn right, you will. Now get them jeans in the wash."

Lucas attempts to take a step past her, but she places her hand on his chest to take a good look at his jeans.

"Hold on. What the hell kinda mud did you fall in anyhow?"

Lucas stands speechless in fear he's been caught and shrugs.

Donna frowns. "You know what? I don't even care. Now get 'em off and in the wash. Then get back out here and wipe this shit up."

"Yes, ma'am," Lucas says with a huge weight lifted from his shoulders as he hurries off.

"At least he's got that boy behavin' a little better," Donna says to herself as she slides a cigarette from a pack and tosses it into her mouth, still tired of Lucas and all his bullshit but feeling slightly gratified that the deputy seems to have had some effect on his attitude.

CHAPTER 14

THE BREAKING POINT

In her kitchen, Karen waits for the timer to ding, signaling a TV dinner is cooked in the oven. In a daze, she watches as the timer counts down. Her concentration is broken by the sound of Abby's laughter from the living room. After a somber look in that direction, she lets her eyes wander to a cabinet above the refrigerator, and she moves toward it. She opens the cabinet, reaches inside, and pulls down a bottle of rum, giving the label a glance before placing the bottle on the counter.

Taking a glass from another cabinet and placing it near the bottle, Karen pauses for a moment and then turns her head back to the open cabinet, her mind wandering. On her tiptoes, she reaches back into the cabinet as far as she can. Her eyes widen the second her fingertips come in contact with what she's searching for. Her feet settle back to the floor as she methodically lowers a revolver from above. Her eyes pour over the weapon, and her thumb strokes the grip.

Ding!

Karen jolts at the sound of the timer, snapping back from wherever her thoughts had led her. She promptly replaces the gun and gives it a quick shove back to the rear of the cabinet.

Kicked back on her couch with a TV tray in front of her, Abby laughs at the television without a care in the world. Karen enters the room, TV dinner in hand, and places it on the tray in front of Abby. She slides forward to the edge of the couch, never letting her eyes leave the television but still acknowledging her mother.

"Thanks, Mommy."

"Uh-huh."

Though physically in the room, Karen, appearing worn and taxed, has mentally checked out. She's confident she has no real power or control over her own daughter or even her own life. She's tried for as many years as she can remember to do what she thinks will be best for her daughter, but she's failing. They seem to be headed straight down the path she so eagerly moved away from.

Karen leaves the room only to reenter a few moments later with a small glass filled with rum and ice. She props herself up against the entryway, takes a few sips, and watches the sweet version of her child that she wishes were the only version. Abby laughs and giggles at *Happy Days*, her favorite television show, happy as anyone could want their child to be.

Sensing her mother's presence, Abby briefly breaks from her show and acknowledges her.

"Whatcha doin', Mommy?"

"Just thinking about when you were young. How I used to hold you and keep you safe, how I used to think that no matter what happened in this world, I'd always be there to protect you," Karen says softly.

"Whatcha drinking?"

"Nothing, honey."

"It looks like alcohol," says Abby, causing Karen to glance down at her drink. "I learned in school that alcohol can kill you."

"A lot of things can kill you, Abby," says Karen, taking another sip.

"You're so funny." Abby allows the television to reclaim her attention.

"Where's your necklace?" asks Karen.

Abby's head whips back toward her. "Why?" She's irritated by the inquisition.

"I haven't seen you wear it the past few days; that's all."

"It's safe." Abby glares at Karen, who gives a fabricated smile and nods.

Abby steadily rotates her head back to the television, but her eyes stay on Karen until she's sucked back in by her show. Forgetting about Karen, she giggles, slipping back to the upbeat, oblivious Abby whom Karen wishes she would always be. Karen sips again and lowers her drink, taking one last, sorrowful look at her daughter in the way she wishes to remember her.

CHAPTER 15

THE MASK REVEALED

Sitting on the edge of his couch, Lucas hunches over the coffee table, which is covered in art supplies, dips a paintbrush into a can of red paint, and moves the brush to his artwork. He casually leans back and observes, pleased with his work thus far, though it's not quite finished. He spontaneously jumps from his seat and runs into his kitchen. He returns with a pair of scissors, plops back on the couch, and continues his project, cutting away at it.

"Lucas! Where are my scissors?" Donna asks from another room.

Lucas temporarily pauses, lifting his head at the sound of his mother's voice, and then he looks back down and hurries to finish before she enters and finds him using her good scissors on what she's sure to think is nothing but another one of his failures.

"Are you listening to me, Lucas?" Donna's frustration is growing. "Lucas? Goddamn it! Why the hell are there potatoes all over the floor in here?"

Donna steps into the living room to find Lucas with the scissors, cutting away and continuing to ignore her. As she gets ready to unleash her fury on him, a dark blurred figure sweeps across the room behind her.

"I'm sick and tired of you doing whatever the hell it is you feel like. This is the kinda shit that reminds me of your good-for-nothin' father."

Lucas, no longer fearful but furious at his mother and her consistent belittling and reminders of how worthless and useless he is, continues to ignore her. Donna sees him bristle, though, and she feeds off his reaction.

"That's right, you little shit. You're just like him. Look at you. You're even a slob like him. What the hell kind of mess is this anyhow?"

Loathing his mother and her comments, Lucas has had enough and rises from the couch.

"I'll show you."

He lifts his masterpiece from the coffee table. It's a black burlap sack with eyeholes cut into it and a red frowning face that drips paint at the corners of the frown.

"This is what you spend your time doing?" asks Donna.

Lucas raises the bag, slips it over his head, and adjusts it so he's able to see. This infuriates Donna past her threshold. Ready to explode at Lucas, she fails to notice the figure now standing motionless behind her. Without a word, Lucas watches in silence as the figure closes in on his mother.

"You piece of shit," Donna says to begin her rant.

The figure swings with the Louisville Slugger. Lucas's eyes close as blood splatters his mask and the portions of his eyes left uncovered. The bat has made contact with the back of Donna's skull, sending her face first to the floor. Lucas's eyes reopen, and he sees blood pool around her head. He stares at her inanimate body.

No tears are shed on this day.

CHAPTER 16

ENOUGH IS ENOUGH

On the edge of her bed, Abby laces up her black Converse high-tops. A small half-packed suitcase is lying open behind her on the bed. A knock at her bedroom door freezes her, laces in hand. Karen presses the door open and steps into the room, her eyes filled with tears, the revolver in her hand, and her finger on the trigger. Abby lets her laces fall and quietly sits up, awaiting her fate.

"It's gonna stop today, Abby," says Karen, no longer crying but showing all the symptoms of a sleepless night and hours spent weeping.

Abby watches her mother's every move as she paces the room, continuing her speech.

"I'm sorry it has to be this way, my sweet Abby. But the hurt, the pain you cause. I can't do it."

Without moving a muscle, Abby intently stares at Karen, taking quick glances at the gun in her hand, trying to decide when the time is right for her to make her move.

"You have no idea the pain I have to deal with, the pain you put me through, and not just me. And I know it's who you are, the way you were born, but the pain, the pain ends today."

Karen stops pacing and faces her daughter. Abby know if she's going to make her move, she needs to do it now. Karen lifts the gun with her finger on the trigger. Abby's eyes widen, and her body trembles. In a flash, Karen presses the gun to the side of her own head and squeezes the trigger.

Bang!

Both Karen and the gun fall to the floor.

Stunned, Abby covers her mouth with her hands as she rises to her feet, taking a minute to comprehend the reality of the situation. Her hands fall to her sides. She's astonished by this unexpected turn of events that now changes her entire world.

"Well, that's gonna make things easy," she says.

With complete disregard for the fact her mother has killed herself before her very eyes, Abby thinks only of the convenient opening it's left for her to make her great escape. She strolls out of her room and down the hall, wiping speckles of blood from her face. Picking up the phone, she begins mustering up some tears as she dials zero for the operator.

She tries to sound hysterical and drum up as much emotion as someone without a conscience can. "Hello? Help please. My mom just shot herself. I live at Four Fifteen Mayfair. No, she's not breathing. I don't know. Please just hurry. Please."

Abby hangs up the phone and immediately becomes calm and composed as she heads back to her blood-covered room. Stepping over her mother's body and grabbing a few more things from her drawer, she throws them into her suitcase and closes it. Packed and ready to go, she glances back at her mother and pauses. She then kneels at her side, brushing the bloodied hair from her mother's face.

"So weak."

At peace with the loss of her mother—and the idea of no longer having to live by her rules or those that govern the rest of the world—Abby is finally free. Suitcase in hand, she exits the room with poise, acting as if she's been there before.

CHAPTER 17

THE GREAT ESCAPE

Lights from police cars and first-response vehicles reflect off Abby's house and the surrounding neighborhood as officers and firefighters secure the area, wrapping their infamous yellow tape around the home. Abby, cuddled up in a standard-issue blanket, waits on the bumper of an ambulance. The local sheriff, fifty-four-year-old Dwayne Moxey, finishes up with another officer, who points him in Abby's direction. The sheriff gives the officer a mournful pat on the back and approaches Abby, who seems heartbroken after what everyone thinks is the tragic death of her mother.

"Abigail?" the sheriff asks, receiving a nod from Abby. "I'm sorry."

Abby hangs her head, able to spark the waterworks, letting more tears fall and continuing to put on a show for everyone at the scene.

Sheriff Moxey continues. "I know this is gonna be hard, and I hate to do this right now, but I have to ask. Did your momma say anything before she... well...did she say anything?"

"She just kept saying how she shouldn't have done it and that she shouldn't have killed them," Abby says as the sheriff writes the information in his notebook. "Then she said she was sorry for what she did and shot herself." Abby begins bawling, barely able to spit out the words. "I don't understand. Why would she do this?"

"I've seen a lot of things over the years I've been doin' this, and all I can tell you is that sometimes people just aren't who they seem to be."

A paramedic and his coworker wheel Karen out the front door of her house, with her body covered in a white sheet, as the sheriff consoles Abby.

"Excuse me, Sheriff," the paramedic says, pushing the gurney behind the sheriff and wanting to go inside the ambulance.

"What the hell is wrong with you?" Sheriff Moxey asks, upset at the paramedic's lack of compassion for Abby as they try to shoo her from the door. "Can't you see she's been through enough?"

Head down in her blanket, still in the doorway of the ambulance, Abby lets a smirk slip at the sheriff's comment, knowing that her mother's death has now become her best alibi.

"Is there someone we call for you, sweetheart?" the sheriff asks.

"One of the other policemen already called my grandma. They said she's on her way," Abby says, back to the business of manipulating anyone she can as long as it gets her where she needs to be.

"All right. Well, I'll be right here with you till she gets here."

"It's OK. Ms. Wright said I can wait at her house until she gets here."

"Eh, I don't know." The sheriff hesitates to let young Abby leave the scene without a guardian.

"It would make me feel better if I could be around someone I know," says Abby, putting on her sad face.

"All right, I guess. But I'll be right here in case you need me. Go on, and head over."

"Yes, sir." Abby removes the blanket from her shoulders and hands it to the sheriff.

"You go on ahead and keep that," he says. "And when your grandma gets here, I need you to have her come see me."

"Yes, sir. Thank you." Abby wraps her arms around him, giving him a big hug, trying to soften him up before making her way to Lucas's door.

On Lucas's doorstep, Abby knocks. She scans the street, which is still lined with police and rescue vehicles, hoping she and Lucas can be stealthy enough and quick enough to make their escape without being seen. Lucas cracks his front door, peeking only his head out. He's nervous about opening his door with all the police around, for fear they'll be able to see what's just inside and thus ending his and Abby's journey before it begins.

"Let me in," Abby whispers.

"What's going on over there?" Lucas asks, keeping the door tight against his body.

"Just open it."

"OK," Lucas says, cringing.

Abby throws on her mournful face before turning back to the sheriff and giving a wave. He returns the wave, watching closely as Abby pushes her way into Lucas's house, squeezing through the barely open door. Lucas closes the door behind her and locks it. He turns back to find Abby gawking as Donna's lifeless, blood-soaked body on the floor.

"Perfect," Abby says, now having to do even less work.

"What do you mean *perfect*?" Lucas asks, accepting his mother's death yet not quite approving of Abby's nonchalant attitude toward it.

"I'll have to explain later. We don't exactly have a lot of time right now, so go grab your stuff so we can get out of here." She knows it's only a matter of time before the sheriff feels the need to come check on her.

"Where?"

"We're running away. Remember?"

"I know that, but where to?"

"We'll have to figure it out later. We don't have a lot of time." Abby hurries toward Lucas's bedroom, having to step over Donna's corpse.

With a small misstep, Abby slips in Donna's blood and almost falls on top of her. Lucas reacts quickly and reaches out to grab and steady Abby. She lets out a giggle at what she thinks is a humorous close call, but she controls her reaction after spotting the scowl on Lucas's face.

"Sorry." Abby says.

Back on her feet, Abby follows Lucas as he heads to his room. He rummages through his drawers and dirty laundry, grabs handfuls of clothes, and shoves them into paper Piggly Wiggly grocery bags as fast as he can while Abby peeks through the blinds and across the way to her bedroom window.

She sees flashbulbs illuminate her room and the shadows of investigators move across her blinds as they analyze the crime scene.

"I can't really see, but I think the sheriff's still outside, so we'll have to be careful on our way out."

"We can use the back door."

Abby lets the blinds snap shut and follows Lucas to the back door. He slowly opens it and cautiously peeks out, surveying the area and making sure they can make a clean break for the woods without being seen.

"It's clear," he says, waving for Abby to follow him out.

"Wait."

"What?"

"I forgot my suitcase."

"We can't do anything about it now. Let's go."

Piggly Wiggly bags in hand, Lucas and Abby sprint back to the woods and enter the tree line. Lucas pauses, glancing back one last time, knowing his life will never be the same or be as unbearable as the time he's spent there. As he stands looking back at his former life, he spots the sheriff walking between the homes, inspecting Abby's house from the outside. Lucas jumps behind a tree at the edge of the woods. He leans from behind it, watching the sheriff as he bends down near the garden hose, grabs a handful of dirt, and shakes it in his palm. The sheriff lifts the dirt to his nose and takes a whiff before tossing it back to the ground and wiping it from his hands.

The sheriff stands, studies the area, and roams between the houses. He spots something protruding from under the house, so he crouches down and pulls Lucas's bloodied shirt from its hiding place.

"That's not gonna be good," Lucas says.

He grabs Abby by the hand and drags her through the woods and away from the scene on their way to anywhere but here.

⚔

Abby's home, surrounded with yellow police tape, lies dormant except for the sheriff, who's resting his rump on the hood of his police car while flipping through the pages of his notebook. He looks at his watch, checks the time, and then gazes back at Lucas's house. He flips his notebook shut, thrusts himself off his patrol car, and makes his way to Lucas's door to check on Abby, wondering what could be taking her grandmother so long.

On the front porch, the sheriff solidly knocks on the door, scanning the area around Lucas's porch while he waits. After a second knock that doesn't receive an answer, he begins feeling uneasy, fearing there may be something awry. Stepping off the porch and peeking through the window, he catches a glimpse of Donna lying on the floor, soaked in blood. He reaches for the doorknob, only to find it's locked. He takes a step back and kicks the door, breaking it open at the latch. On the floor in front of him lies Donna.

Sheriff Moxey is more concerned about the missing children. He presses the button on his walkie-talkie.

"Sheriff Moxey to dispatch."

"Go for dispatch," the operator says.

"We're gonna need to get all available units back out to Mayfair Avenue. It's Four Seventeen this time. Looks like we got us another body." He pulls the mic away from his mouth for a moment before placing it back. "We also have two missing children, both age twelve, one boy, one girl. We're gonna need an APB and checkpoints on all roads within the next, oh, let's say thirty miles or so."

"Roger that, Sheriff."

Standing above Donna's body, the sheriff thinks about how he's at fault for sending such a sweet young girl who'd just lost her mother straight into the hands of someone who's now surely her captor and who may be some sort of serial killer.

CHAPTER 18

Not So Fast

On an Alabama backcountry road barely lit by Abby's and Lucas's flashlights, the two runaways stroll side by side with their flashlights and Piggly Wiggly bags in their hands. They kick a few rocks down the center of a beat-up blacktop road.

"How much farther are we gonna have to walk?" Lucas asks, exhausted and hungry.

"Someone's bound to drive past soon. Besides, who'd leave two kids on the side of the road in the middle of the night?"

"We haven't seen a car in forever. I don't think anyone's coming."

Discouraged, Lucas picks up a rock and chucks it down the street. Abby laughs, watching the rock bounce down the blacktop and off to the gravel shoulder.

"What's so funny?" Lucas says, unable to find the humor in much at this point.

"That's what started all this," Abby says, still chuckling.

"What's that?"

"You throwing rocks."

Thinking back over their previous adventures, Lucas loosens up, letting a small smile escape as they continue their trek farther into the unknown.

"Hey, look," Lucas says, running ahead with a skip in his step as he spots the taillights of a vehicle up ahead. "There's someone up here."

Abby darts off in an attempt to keep pace with Lucas. He begins to slow as he approaches a Volkswagen van off to the side of the road; its lights are on, and music is blaring. Lucas throws his arm out to stop Abby, pointing to the passenger's side of the vehicle. A blond woman lies sprawled out on the ground, half hanging in the doorway.

"Now what?" Lucas whispers.

"Do you know how to drive?"

"What?"

"Well, if she's already dead, she's not gonna need her van."

Although still not as accepting of death as Abby is, he does agree the woman will no longer need the van, and they are in a position where this may be the break they were looking for. Once again, he's on board.

"Let's go," he says as he slowly approaches, looking for any other signs of life.

As they close in on the VW, Lucas spots a man's body lying on the ground a few feet away. Lucas stops. Abby, with her eyes on the woman, bumps into Lucas, who clutches his chest, about to freak out.

"Sorry," Abby says.

"What do you think?" Lucas asks, whispering as he scans the area.

From behind, they hear footsteps approach. When they turn around, they see a man with a black burlap sack on his head who's holding a wooden Louisville Slugger and standing only a few feet away. He towers over them. Abby, who's willing to do anything to save her newfound love, places herself in front of Lucas.

"Please don't hurt him," she says.

"Lucas, get in the van," the masked man says, raising the bat toward Lucas.

Lucas moves from behind Abby, leaving her baffled as he climbs into the back seat of the van, as the masked man asked.

"Daddy, how do you know Lucas? And what took you so long to come get us?" Abby asks as Eddie removes the sack from his head, grinning.

"Hop in, and I'll tell you," he says.

Abby throws her arms around her father and makes for the van, kicking the blond woman's leg from the door before hopping in and slamming the door behind her. Eddie climbs in behind the steering wheel and fires up the engine. Abby's eyes sparkle with excitement, for she's finally able to be back at her father's side.

"It smells funny in here," says Lucas.

"Hey. Cookies," says Abby. She opens the tin and finds only marijuana. "Never mind. So, tell me already."

"So, two weeks ago…" Eddie starts his story as he shifts the van into gear and tears off into the night.

CHAPTER 19

THE NOT SO STRANGER

As Eddie drives the VW van down the backcountry roads, he fills Abby in on his run-ins with Lucas after his arrival in Alabama. The first encounter had been when Lucas and Abby were heading to the school for the first time, as Abby glanced across the street at Eddie when he was passing by on the opposite side.

In the grocery store on the bread aisle, Lucas smashed the loaves of bread as Eddie pushed his cart into the aisle, passing Lucas on his way to the cash register. Again, they met at the register. Lucas had stared while Eddie returned the coin Donna dropped.

As Abby prepared to cut Daniel loose from the tree, she glanced off into the woods and received verification from her father as he ran his index finger across his throat, letting Abby know that Daniel must die. Eddie watched as she killed Daniel and then joined Lucas and ran off, leaving Daniel's body for anyone to find.

After Daniel's murder, Lucas helped Abby into her bedroom window but couldn't stop worrying about the body and the possibility of it being found, so he grabbed a shovel from his house and returned to the scene of the crime. As he approached the body, shovel in hand, he tapped the ground in a few places, looking for a good spot to dig. After an hour, he stood in a hole barely deep enough to bury his report card. Out of nowhere, a flashlight clicked on, blinding Lucas and leaving him wondering whether he'd been caught. Eddie stood a few feet away, holding the light. He then lowered it, allowing Lucas to see his face. Lucas recognized him instantly as the stranger from the grocery store, and the wooden Louisville Slugger in his hand was his own.

"You shouldn't leave your things where anyone could take them," Eddie said, looming over Lucas as he stood in his half-dug hole. Lucas tried to take a step back but tripped on the edge of the hole and fell on his rear. The pendant hanging from his neck glistened in the light of the flashlight. "Where did you get that?" Eddie asked.

"I know you. You're the guy from the grocery store."

"I asked you where you got that."

"It was given to me by someone special. You'll have to kill me before I give it to you."

Eddie glared at Lucas, who clutched the pendant. He stepped toward Lucas and stood over him, with the bat slung over his shoulder. Lucas shivered. Eddie tossed the bat onto the ground next to Lucas, bent down, picked up Daniel's body, and threw it over his shoulder.

"Grab it, and let's go," he said, pointing to the bat.

Lucas, thoroughly confused, stared, afraid to move, unsure what this stranger was doing in the woods and why he wasn't concerned about the dead body draped over his shoulder.

"Look. That hole's never gonna work. Now pick up the bat, and let's go, if you want my help," Eddie said.

"I don't understand why you're helping me." Lucas grabbed the bat and followed him through the woods.

"I'm not. I'm helping the person who gave you that necklace."

"Abby?" Lucas stopped in his tracks.

"She's my daughter. Now keep walking." Eddie stopped long enough to get Lucas back on track.

"Wait. I thought she said you were dead."

"Is that what she told you?"

"Not exactly," Lucas said, thinking back to an earlier conversation.

"Do you see me with her?"

"No."

"Then shut up, and keep walking."

Lucas continued following him through the woods, still trying to process why Abby wouldn't let on that her father was apparently not only alive and well but also watching her and Lucas's every move. A few minutes into the hike, Lucas got bored and began swinging his bat, hitting brush and small trees, causing Eddie to stop.

"Maybe we don't make so much noise," Eddie said.

"Sorry," Lucas said, trying his best not to do anything rash to cause the strange man who was claiming to be Abby's father—and carrying a corpse over his shoulder—to become upset. Apparently the man didn't have a problem with ending a life, including that of a child.

As they hiked onward, Lucas began recognizing the area, and it hit him as Daniel's cabin came into view.

"Why are we here?" he whispered.

"To fix your mistakes." Eddie dropped Daniel's body onto the ground. "Now wait here."

Eddie took the bat from Lucas's hand and maneuvered through the woods to the front door of Mr. Stetson's cabin. Lucas half hid himself behind a tree, avidly watching to see what Eddie had planned. Eddie rang the doorbell, stepped off the porch just to the side of the door, and lifted the bat to his shoulder, ready to swing.

"You goddamn kids are gonna be sorry when I find out which one of you keeps pulling this shit," Mr. Stetson yelled as he opened the door of his cabin and extended the tip of his shotgun out of the front door.

Eddie swung the bat.

The bat cracked against Mr. Stetson's face, making him collapse back into the house with his feet lying in the doorway. Eddie stepped inside, straddled Mr. Stetson, and furiously rained the bat down on him until he was satisfied the job was done.

In the doorway, Eddie rose, out of breath; grabbed Mr. Stetson's legs; and pulled him inside and out of view. He then came back outside and headed straight to Lucas, blood-soaked bat in hand. Lucas was astonished at Eddie's ability to kill with ease.

"Is there anyone else who knows you've been out here?" Eddie asked.

"No…" Lucas answered with hesitation.

"Are you sure?" Eddie lifted Daniel's body from the ground and tossed it over his shoulder.

"Yeah. Well, he doesn't know it was me and Abby, but Deputy Morgan asked if I was the one who broke the window," Lucas said, following Eddie back to the cabin.

"Anybody else?" he asked, growing impatient and glancing over at the broken window as he entered the cabin, carrying Daniel's body.

Reappearing from the cabin without the body, he stopped himself within feet of Lucas, watching his mannerisms closely. Lucas lowered his head, knowing who else might know about the window.

"Who is it?" Eddie asked, already having an idea.

"My mom."

"We'll worry about the deputy first. And since this is your mess, you're gonna help. Here's what I'm gonna need from you."

Lucas nodded, listening intently to every word of Eddie's plan to fix the predicament.

⅄

At the front door of Daniel's cabin, Lucas stood next to the deputy, his body tense in anticipation of what was about to happen. Lucas closed his eyes and heard the familiar crack of the wooden bat striking the deputy. Lucas gradually opened his eyes and gazed at him as he sluggishly squirmed and gasped for air, blood covering his head as he fought to stay alive. Eddie stepped forward next to Lucas, taking pleasure in watching the deputy struggle.

Eddie extended the bat to Lucas, placing it across his chest and suggesting Lucas take over from here. Lucas glanced down at the bat and then back to Eddie, who gave Lucas a slow nod. Lucas's hands wrapped tightly around the bat as Eddie passed the figurative baton to the next generation of killer.

"Good," Eddie said.

Lucas inhaled deeply through his nose and exhaled out of his mouth, preparing for the chore at his feet. The deputy, looking into Lucas's eyes, shook his head no, trying to persuade him to have some sympathy. Lucas balked, unsure he could go through with the act until he heard the snap of the deputy's gun holster and spotted his hand on his gun.

Lucas broke.

Instantaneously the bat flew toward the deputy, crashing into his head. The deputy fell unconscious as Lucas continued to swing away, becoming more and more enraged with every swing. Eddie stepped in, placing his hand on Lucas's shoulder and holding him back to prevent him from taking another swing.

"You've done good," he said.

Unable to take his eyes from the carnage that was once the deputy's face, Lucas started becoming misty eyed and overwhelmed with emotion. Eddie pulled him in for a hug.

"I'm proud of you. You did the right thing."

Lucas broke down, hugging Eddie tightly and crying from the surge of hate and hostility, as well as because of the respect and heartfelt praise he'd been lacking in his life and was now getting from Eddie.

"Me and Abby are your family now."

Lucas's eyes pierced through the black burlap sack covering his head as Eddie continued pounding Donna with the bat.

When the job was done, Eddie looked at Lucas, waiting to see how he reacted to the incident.

"You OK?" Eddie asked.

Lucas removed the sack from his head, his eyes fixated on his mother. With a look of disgust and hatred still brewing, he nodded.

"It's her own fault," he said.

Bringing his eyes back to Eddie, he lifted the mask and held it out to him.

"I made this for you. I thought you could use it."

Eddie took the mask and smiled, placing a hand on Lucas's head and ruffling his hair.

Lucas was delighted as the praise for his misbehaviors continued.

CHAPTER 20

STICK A FORK IN 'EM

In the dead of night on a backcountry road, the Volkswagen van idles, and two patrol cars are parked diagonally, blocking the road ahead. Two policemen lean against the open doors of their cars, guns drawn and pointed at the van. Spotlights from the cruisers shine through the windshield and into Eddie's eyes. Abby, who's in the passenger's seat pulls her hair back into a ponytail. Red-and-blue lights flicker off the van and the surroundings.

"Put your hands where we can see them," one officer yells.

"Help us!" Abby screams.

"Please help us!" Lucas says, following Abby's lead.

"Driver, keep your hands where we can see them," the other officer yells, prompting Eddie to raise his hands above the steering wheel.

"Please do something…please," Abby shouts.

"Children, slowly exit the vehicle, and walk toward us. Driver, keep your hands where we can see them."

Abby opens the passenger's side door, and Lucas slides open the rear door. Both kids exit the van slowly and cautiously.

"Do not move, Driver, or we will shoot. Do you understand?" the officer asks, still posted behind his door.

Eddie nods as Abby and Lucas run to the police, free of their captor. Abby lunges at one of the officers, wrapping her arms around him, and Lucas stands behind the other.

"Thank you, thank you," Abby says in tears.

"Get back," says the officer to Abby in an attempt to shoo her, but she holds tight. "You have to let go, precious. Please go wait in the car. You'll be safe there."

Abby and Lucas climb into the cruisers and out of the way. The policemen now turn their attention back to Eddie, whose hands are still up.

"Driver, slowly reach your hands out the window, and open the door from the outside."

Eddie places both hands out of the van's window of the van, puts one on the handle, and leaves the other in the air. He pulls the handle and pops the door open, gradually transitioning from the driver's seat to the street while holding both hands high.

"Now drop to your knees, keeping your hands above your head."

Eddie's face goes from expressionless to smug as he deliberately lets his hands lower to his sides.

"Get your hands up; get 'em up!" the officer says.

The two officers step away from their doors and approach Eddie, both putting one foot in front of the other, keeping their guns extended and their fingers on the triggers, continuing their march.

"This is your last chance. Get 'em over your head. We will shoot you," the officer continues to explain.

"I said up," the other officer says.

Both officers hold their positions, gripping their guns tightly.

Eddie winks.

Two shots ring out, and Eddie flinches, his eyes fluttering. One of the officers looks down at the blood soaking through his shirt as he falls to his knees. Before he fully slips into unconsciousness, he catches a glimpse of the other officer, who's facedown on the road, just as his body meets the black-top. Lucas stands behind him, holding the officer's standard-issue shotgun from the patrol car. Beside him, Abby holds the other officer's shotgun at her side; there's smoke wafting from the barrel.

"I told you it would work," Abby says confidently.

"I knew you guys could do it," Eddie says as the trio regroups.

"In it together," he says, giving Abby a hug and Lucas a pat on the head.

"In it together," Abby and Lucas say simultaneously.

Lucas, Abby, and Eddie get back into the van for their escape. They drive off the side of the road, around the patrol cars, and into the night. The bodies of the two fallen officers lie silent as the lights of the patrol cars reflect off the surroundings.

⋏

Abby and Lucas lie asleep in the back of the van as Eddie drives the back-country roads, trying to put as much distance between them and that small town as fast as he can. The radio fades in and out with static as he adjusts the knob to the next clear station.

He catches a news report. "In this small Alabama town, where six people are dead and two children are still missing, police urge anyone with information to call their local authorities immediately—"

Click.

Eddie turns the volume knob off as the van approaches a road sign at a fork in the road:

Montgomery 47 miles →
← Mobile 175 miles

He steers the van to the right and drives off until the taillights fade into the dark.

⋏

At the same road sign just minutes later, Sheriff Dwayne Moxey sits parked in his car, staring at the sign, pondering the path of the killer and the missing children. He flicks his blinker, takes a left turn, and drives into the night.

The End

Author Biography

Gunnar E. Garrett Jr. is an award-winning screenwriter with a combined forty-five nominations and wins in competitions and film festivals around the world.

Gunnar was born and raised in Modesto, California, and joined the military after high school. After a twelve-year career in the US Air Force and then the National Guard, he began to spend most of his time with his five daughters. It was his second oldest who sparked his passion for screenplays when she began showing interest in the film industry.

Gunnar began writing with the goal of creating a leading role for his daughter, Madison Mae, and with his most recent award-winning screenplay, Riley's Rainbow (set for production in fall 2017), he has succeeded. He has even begun acting himself but continues in his commitment to writing excellent screenplays and, now, novel adaptations.

www.ingramcontent.com/pod-product-compliance
Lightning Source LLC
Chambersburg PA
CBHW070941250626
47159CB00009B/3331